I'm Pretty Sure You're Gonna Miss Me Ronin McKinsey

I'm Pretty Sure About That Series Book One

M. J. Padgett

MJ Padgett Books LLC

Book Cover by Avery Daisy Book Design

Contents

One

"**T**his is a bad, bad idea, Hazel. It's too much." Sara glanced up toward the gymnasium ceiling filled with balloons in a rainbow of colors. It was perfect, and I knew Ronin would love it.

It was our first anniversary. One year since he'd kissed me as we watched a rainbow fade after a huge thunderstorm. It was magical, and I wanted to recreate the scene. I ordered 365 multi-colored balloons, one for every day we were together, and filled them with helium to create a rainbow in the gym. I did not, however, anticipate the lovely lady at the party supply shop would accidentally send 3,650 balloons. *Eh, what's a few thousand more?*

"Nonsense. He's going to love it," I said, waving her off as I released another bundle of balloons. They floated happily to the ceiling, blending with the other 2,975 we'd already set free. Sara shook her head and continued filling balloons with helium.

"Fine then, but it's your funeral." She was dramatic. Sara was *always* dramatic, always telling me to pull back a little, but I couldn't. Who could pull back when they were in love? Who didn't shower the love of their life with affection every chance they got? Of course, our first anniversary had to be amazing. It had to be over-the-top amazing, just like Ronin.

"We're going to be here forever." She groaned again and adjusted the skirt of her cheer uniform. It was getting late, and the guys would be finished with practice soon. We still had a few hundred balloons to fill, but I knew we could get it done. I had confidence our efforts would be rewarded and Ronin would fall in love with me all over again.

I might have been a touch over-confident about how quickly we were moving, though. After a moment, I heard the tell-tale signs the guys had finished practice—squeaky cleats on the gymnasium floor and a half-dozen soccer balls rolling in from the double side doors.

"Oh, fiddlesticks," I said. I dropped the handful of deflated balloons I had stuffed in my hand and shoved the box under the bleachers. Sara didn't have a chance to disappear before the guys crowded through the gym door.

Coach Peters saw us and nodded a polite hello before ordering the guys to shower. He was always a little cranky, but he was also my uncle, so he tried harder with me. He disappeared into his office and closed the door while the guys mumbled about him being a jerk. When the team was out of sight again, we went back to filling the balloons.

We moved a lot faster. Many of them were sadly underinflated, but they blended in with the full balloons that covered the entire gymnasium ceiling. When there were only a few left, Sara turned off her helium tank and pushed it back into the corner.

"I've gotta get home, or my Mom's gonna freak. Call me later?" she asked.

I nodded, working quickly to fill the last few balloons before Ronin came out of the locker room. "Sure thing, but it might be late. I've been thinking a lot, and I think maybe tonight might be *the* night," I said.

She stopped short, her gym bag half on her shoulder and her eyes wide. "The night? Like *the* night?"

"Yeah, why not? I'll be eighteen in a few weeks, and I love him."

"Right, but just because you love him doesn't mean you should—" A door slammed, startling us both. "Just... just be sure it's what you want, okay? You always said you wanted to wait until marriage."

I hugged her and helped her pull her heavy bag onto her shoulder. "I know, but... I don't know, it just feels like the right time, but I promise I'll think about it more."

"Please do. Anyway, I need to hurry." She rushed toward the door with a little jog.

"Love you!"

"Love you, too!" she shouted over her shoulder.

I glanced down at my uniform, a little wrinkled from working but still cute as can be. I cleared the area, picked up the last of our mess, and waited for Ronin. I was excited for many reasons. I couldn't believe, even after a year, that I was dating Ronin McKinsey. Captain of the soccer team, gorgeous, straight-A student—he was my perfect boyfriend. Sara always said it was cliché, the cheer captain dating the soccer captain, but I thought it was adorable. Who wouldn't? After every game, he took me for ice cream and cake, *our thing.* And what guy didn't love having his girlfriend cheer for him from the sidelines? It was perfect. He was perfect, and we were the perfect couple.

"What the...?" Tanner Gibson gazed at the ceiling, taking in all 3,650 balloons. "Did a bag of jelly beans blow up in here?"

I giggled at him and said, "No, silly. They're for Ronin. It's our anniversary."

"Oh," he said. "How could I ever forget?" His tone was a bit sarcastic for my liking, but then, he always was sort of a jerk. He yelled over his shoulder and pointed toward the ceiling. "Hey, Tee, come get a look at this!"

Terrence Gordon and several other players filed out of the locker room, following Tanner's pointing finger. Tee, Ronin's best friend, gazed upward and let his jaw fall open. Tee and I had always gotten along well, even when I tore Ronin away from their guy's nights. He looked around the ceiling, every inch covered in bright-colored balloons. His gaze lowered and settled on me, but rather than his usual cheery smile, his face held a look of concern.

His concern was the last thing on my mind when I caught Ronin staring at the balloons. "What the…"

"Looks like your girl's been busy. Tell me, when's the wedding, McKinsey?" Tanner asked.

"Shut up, Tanner." Ronin's face was red, and his lips turned down into a scowl.

"Aw, are you afraid it's gonna hurt your tough-guy reputation? I'm afraid that ship has sailed, my friend. You're what we call whipped, Ronin. Whipped, I say." Tanner laughed maniacally as he waltzed out the door. A few of the other guys followed, also snickering. I didn't understand. Didn't their girlfriends do nice things for them?

Terrence gave me one last look, then picked up his gym bag and walked out, leaving me alone with a frustrated boyfriend. Ronin ran his hands through his hair and groaned. "Hazel, what is this?"

I walked to the other side of the gym with a purposeful spring in my step. He was upset, but I could fix it. Once I told him the idea, he'd love it. He'd take me to dinner, and, well, whatever happened after that would be great, too.

"Balloons, you know, for our anniversary," I said excitedly. "I wanted to recreate the rainbow we kissed under, so I ordered 365 rainbow-colored balloons to release in the gym for you."

"This is more than 365 balloons, Hazel!" His raised voice echoed in the vacant gym.

"Well, yeah, see, there was an accident when I ordered, and she sent me 3,650 balloons. Since I had them, I figured—"

"There are 3,650 balloons up there? How are you going to get them all down before tomorrow?" he asked, frustration lacing his tone. I thought he'd like it. Why was he behaving as if I'd punched him in the face?

"Tomorrow?"

"Yes, Hazel, tomorrow! The biggest basketball game of the season! The deciding game for playoffs, Hazel! Coach Conroy is going to murder you!"

"You don't have to shout, babe. I'll figure something out, I'm sure. It's no big deal. I'll just come in early tomorrow and..." I gazed at the ceiling. *What would I do?*

"Ugh, Hazel." Ronin dropped his head and sighed.

"I thought you would be happy."

"Did it ever occur to you to just buy seven balloons? One for each color of the rainbow?" he asked, looking back at me. He was no longer frustrated, but he wasn't happy either.

"N-no. I... I guess I could have done that, but I thought—"

"Did you? Did you think, Hazel? Because if you'd taken a second to think about this insanity, then maybe you'd have realized how embarrassing it is!" He'd never yelled at me before, and his tone was beginning to worry me.

"If you don't like it, it's fine. I'll just take them down. It's not such a big deal, really," I said, trying to come up with a way to quickly deflate the balloons before he popped a gasket over them.

"It's 3,650 balloons, woman! How on earth did you even get all of them up there?" he asked.

"Sara and I—"

"Oh, right, Sara. Did she even bother to *try* to talk you out of this, or does she enjoy watching you make a fool of yourself?" he asked as he dropped his gym bag with a clunk. "For a best friend, she sure does spend a lot of time watching you do stupid stuff without trying to stop you."

I took a step back, startled by his words. I didn't want to cry, but it was difficult to keep the tears from falling. I managed to wipe them away when he lowered his head. I coughed, trying to break the silence, but it only got me in deeper trouble.

"Why? Why do you constantly push everything over the top? Why can't you be like a normal girlfriend?" Ronin asked. He jerked his bag up, settled the strap on his shoulder, grumbled, and walked away.

"Where are you going? It's our anniversary, Ronin! I was trying to do something nice for you!" I shouted at his back.

He turned and yelled back. "You want to do something nice for me? Go home, Hazel. Go home and figure out how you're going to get those balloons down." He slammed the door behind him. The sound of it echoed in the gym, even with the giant balloon buffer.

I let the tears fall then, embarrassed and insulted. Those stupid guys. If it weren't for them teasing him, Ronin would have loved it. If it weren't for them, Ronin and I would have been on our way to dinner that very second. I grabbed my own bag and hoisted it over my shoulder. At the door, I glanced up once more. How was I going to get them all down before the game?

I sighed, leaving it to worry about when I got home. I flipped the light switch off, darkening the gym. A balloon popped, and it scared the poo out of me. Maybe, with any luck, they would all pop by morning, just like my heart. I could come back in the morning and pick up their little skeletons and be done with it. Not much to do about the popped heart, though.

I pulled into the driveway of my family home a little after dusk and parked beside my sister's best friend's car. Dizzy was almost always at our house, which I didn't mind, but Sara wasn't her biggest fan. Dizzy was loud and a little obnoxious, but I found her to be funny and endearing.

Rose met me at the door, her phone pressed against her ear. "Okay, yeah. Thanks for letting me know." She ended the call and slipped her phone in her pocket.

"What was that about?" I asked, observing her overly worried face as I got out of my car. For a moment, I considered getting back in and making a few more rounds through the neighborhood just to... I don't know, kill time before my sister said whatever it was I just *knew* was bad news.

"Um... I think we should talk, maybe in my room?" Rose rarely let me in her room. We were close, but she was messy, and I was fanatical about keeping my room neat and organized. I couldn't help myself. Whenever I entered her room, I instinctively started cleaning it instead of paying attention to her.

"Oh, okay. Isn't Denise here?" I walked through the door and saw Dizzy sitting at the kitchen island talking to my mother, who was working her magic over the stove.

"Yeah, it'll be fine. Mom's teaching her how to make pasta." Dizzy gave me a faint smile when I passed, but it was forced. Dizzy never forced a smile. *What is happening?*

Rose closed the door behind us and paced the floor. I began tossing her dirty laundry into her hamper while I waited for her to decide how to say what she wanted to say.

"Don't do that. Those are clean in there," Rose said, pulling the dirty items out of the basket.

"Why are they in your basket?" I asked, moving on to organize her bookshelf instead.

"Hazel, stop it." She took her books from my hands and practically shoved me down on her bed. I yelped when I sat on something hard. I reached under my bum and pulled out a fork.

"Honestly, Rose, you really need to get this mess in order," I said, tossing the fork onto her desk where the collection of dishes there grew something resembling a biology project gone horribly wrong.

"Hazel!" I gave her my attention, but the fuzzy monster growing on her week-old pizza scraps made it difficult.

"What's wrong, Rose?"

She sighed and said, "Ronin's gonna break up with you."

I popped up from the bed. "What? Who told you that? Why? When?"

"It doesn't matter how I know, but my source is solid. What were you thinking, Hazel? Filling the gym with balloons? It had to take, like, a thousand balloons to fill it!"

"Try 3,650," I said, falling back onto the bed.

Her eyes popped. "Oh, Hazel." She flopped on the bed beside me and took my hand in hers. "I know we're twins, but even I don't get you sometimes. I love you, but I don't get you. Maybe it's because we're not identical, who knows, but can you please tell me why you filled a gym with rainbow balloons?"

"Can you tell me who told you?"

She sighed again. "It was Tee. He felt bad for you, and he called me, hoping I could soften the blow. Ronin just told him a little while ago."

"Wonderful. Now, what do I do?" I asked, not that there was much to do.

"Maybe just pull back? Give him a few days to cool off, and maybe it will work out, okay?"

I knew she was right. Ronin was angry, but he couldn't stay mad forever, not over some silly balloons. "Okay, maybe you're right."

The problem with Hazel Simmons pulling back was that I didn't know how.

I left Rose's room already devising a plan to keep Ronin. He just had to remember how good we were together, that's all. He had to remember the great times like the ice cream and cake dates. That was it, the golden ticket. Once I got all the balloons down from the gym ceiling in the morning, I'd give him an ice cream cake with an apology written in icing.

It would work. He would love it, and I would keep my boyfriend.

My wheels turned, and I barely heard my phone dinging as I practiced inscription after inscription, scrapping each one because they were too long to write on a cake. I finally heard the ding and glanced over at the screen. Four missed calls from Sara and three messages.

Sarah

Where are you?

I'm worried, please call me!

How did it go?

I silenced the phone, not at all interested in explaining to my best friend why I wasn't enjoying dinner with my boyfriend. Maybe she was right? Maybe 3,650 balloons were a few too many. Still, I couldn't think that way. I had to look toward tomorrow and figure out what I would say to make things better.

I scribbled another inscription, made a few quick changes, and smiled. It was good. Perfect.

I opened my laptop and pulled up the website for the local bakery. There were so many to choose from, but I settled on what I knew was Ronin's favorite—chocolate cake with strawberry ice cream. I perused the additional options, balloons being one of them. *No, thank you, I've plenty of those. Extra frosting, sprinkles, ah... inscriptions.*

I typed in the message, which luckily fit in the 200-character maximum, and clicked on the submit button. Delivery options... *Geez, how many questions are necessary to order a cake?*

"Hazel! Dinner's ready!" my mother called from downstairs.

"Coming!" I clicked on the little circle beside the *pick-up your order* option, paid, and slammed my computer shut. I smiled and hurried down the stairs, pleased with my plan.

Ronin would be so surprised. Boy, would he be surprised.

Two

I woke extra early the next morning, having over three thousand balloons to somehow retrieve from the ceiling of the gym. I wanted to get it done as quickly as possible. Maybe if they were gone before Ronin arrived, he'd be a little less upset about the entire incident and forgive me faster.

I showered and got dressed, grabbed a protein bar on the way out the door, and drove to school with a plan in mind. I'd borrow a ladder from the janitor, tape a nail to the end of a broomstick, and with any luck, I could harpoon those balloons to death and sweep them off the floor. I pulled into the parking lot, nearly empty, save a half-dozen cars that probably belonged to teachers.

My shoes squeaked in the hall, echoing loudly without it being filled to the brim with teenagers talking and yelling. When I arrived at the gym, I was surprised to see the lights on already. My uncle didn't usually come in until after the first period, his planning period. I opened the double doors and found Tee wobbling on a ladder, trying very hard to reach one of the green balloons that somehow managed to wedge itself between a hanging light and the wall.

The ladder wiggled a little too much, and he toppled from the top rung. I ran toward him as fast as I could and caught him at the last second. Thank goodness he wasn't one of the larger guys on the team, or we would have both splatted on the gymnasium floor. Still, he was heavy, and I dropped him shortly after catching him. He landed with a thud on his butt, but he recovered fast and leaped to his feet.

"Dang, you're freakishly strong for a girl," he said, adjusting his glasses so they weren't askew on his face.

"For a girl?" I asked, somewhat teasing since I knew there was no way Tee meant to insinuate girls could not be strong. "I am a cheer captain. I've had to do some catching in my day, not to mention throwing girls in the air."

"Came out wrong, I swear. I'm just impressed you caught me, and grateful. Thanks, Hazel," he said and climbed the ladder again. "Can you hold it? I almost had that little booger."

"Why are you here? Why are you catching balloons for me?" I asked, steadying the ladder as he climbed. He felt terrible for me, I knew it, but I didn't want the pity.

"Because Ronin was kind of a jerk about this yesterday, and I told him it wouldn't be hard to fix. The problem is, now I must prove it isn't difficult to fix. It turns out it is. I don't know what you're gonna do, Hazel. I've been here an hour, and I've only been able to get like fifty down."

Tee was a real sweetheart, and I made a mental note to do something special to thank him. "Ah, I had an idea on the way here. Hang on." I ran to the janitorial closet in the girls' locker room and quickly found a broom, but no luck with nails. I did find an old screw that had fallen out of one of the door hinges, so I figured that would do just as well since it was sharp. I duct-taped it to the broom and jogged back out the door.

"Here, it's a harpoon." I handed it up to Tee, and he stabbed a few balloons. I caught them as they fell, and it became a sort of game. He'd pop them, and I'd try to catch them until we'd made significant headway. In all, it took another two hours to get most of them down.

My uncle walked in, took in the remainder of the balloons, and said, "Why'd you pop them all? We could have used them for the pre-game pep rally."

I smacked my forehead, wishing I'd thought to ask that before getting up two and a half hours early for school.

Tee descended the ladder, harpoon in hand. "Well, I guess my work here is done, assuming you want to leave the rest?"

"I guess it's fine. Thanks for the help. I really appreciate it, Tee, really. You're Ronin's best friend, so it was really cool of you to step up and help me."

"I'm your friend, too." He shrugged slightly and untaped the screw from the broomstick. "Sometimes, he can be a jerk. You were just trying to be nice, maybe a little overboard, but he still shouldn't have yelled at you for trying to be sweet."

"I'm glad you think so. My sister and Sara think it was nuts," I admitted.

"Well, it was a little nutty, but that doesn't make it *unsweet*. I've gotta get to class. See you at lunch?" He handed me the broom and screw with a little head nod.

"Sure, at lunch." I put the items away and rushed to class after hearing the warning bell. First period was with Sara, and I wasn't looking forward to telling her she was right. She did try to warn me not to blow up so many balloons, but as usual, I ignored her suggestion and plowed ahead.

I slid into my seat moments before the bell rang. Sara was flipping through her textbook when I landed, and she glanced up at me. "Oh, you're here! I missed you this morning. Where were you?"

"With Tee in the gym popping those stupid balloons." I sighed, best to get it over with right up front. "Listen, you were right. It was a bad idea, and I'm sorry I didn't listen to you. Maybe if I had, I wouldn't have gotten into an argument with Ronin last night."

"Oh, Hazel, I'm sorry. I take it that means your anniversary plans were a bust?"

"Definitely. He didn't even want to look at me after Tanner teased him about the balloons, let alone... you know," I said, suddenly glad I hadn't handed my virginity over to Ronin earlier in our relationship. Maybe I didn't want someone so freaked by balloons to be my first. What was I thinking?

"Tanner is an idiot, but I think maybe you would have gotten into the fight anyway. Hazel, I love you, but sometimes the things you do are a bit much. It can really make a person feel smothered." Her statement wasn't intended to hurt me, but it did.

I stuffed my face in the textbook and didn't speak again until class ended. Sara barely noticed she'd hurt my feelings, and by the time class was over, she'd forgotten entirely. "So, have you spoken to him since last night?" she asked.

"No, but I did order him an ice cream cake from Fire and Ice, our place. I'm gonna pick it up after class and deliver it to him myself. I just hope the apology iced on it is enough." I didn't go into the details of what Rose told me. For some reason, I didn't want my best friend to know Ronin intended to break up with me. For all I knew, Ronin might even break it off at school well before I could deliver my apology cake. It made me nervous every time I thought about it, so I had to swallow down the anxiety that tickled my throat.

"Are you sure that's a good idea? Maybe he needs time to cool off before you try to apologize in your typical Hazel way?" she asked.

"Of course, he needs time to cool off. That's why I didn't call him last night. But what harm can come from delivering food as an apology? I'll just drop it off and head home, that's all. He can decide what he wants while he's eating," I reasoned. "And if he's eating an ice cream cake from our place, maybe it will help him remember the good times."

"Wait, why would he need to remember... Hazel, did he break up with you?" I'm not sure why, but her face did not match the concern in her voice. Her voice sounded supportive, concerned, shocked even, but her face appeared downright happy.

"No," I said, "but Tee told Rose he planned to today."

"All the more reason not to bother him. Let him figure it out, then let him come to you. Trust me," she said.

"Maybe you're right. It's too late to cancel the cake, though. Want to come over this afternoon and eat apology cake?" I asked. "Chocolate and strawberry?"

"Sure, why not?" Sara slammed her locker door closed and followed me down the hall. Everywhere we went, people snickered or stared. For goodness sake, balloons in the gym couldn't be *that* funny, but it appeared people couldn't manage to act like adults. A few more people pointed and laughed as we turned the corner, forcing me to wonder if something else had happened... like Ronin telling everyone he planned to break up with me.

"Sara, what is going on?"

"No idea, but it feels like trouble." She looked around, catching people staring and laughing everywhere. I felt like the punchline in a joke I never heard, standing in the middle of the hall with hundreds of eyes on me.

"Hazel!" Rose rushed up to me. "What have you done? I thought we agreed to let Ronin settle down. Why on earth would you send him a singing telegram and a giant cake here at school?"

"What?" I asked, panicking. "I ordered a cake, but I'm supposed to pick it up after school!" A feeling of dread filled my chest as I slid my phone from my pocket. I opened my emails and tapped the confirmation from Fire and Ice. It felt like a million little monkeys were dancing on my chest while I searched for the method of delivery.

"See? Look." I handed my phone to Rose. Sara leaned in and looked over my sister's shoulder.

"Oh, Hazel! You clicked on the wrong button. Look!" Sara said, pointing to the correct button. The little checkbox was behind the option, not in front, so the box I *thought* was intended for pick-up was actually for the singing telegram delivery.

"Who puts the button after the option? Everyone knows it comes before the choice. How could they screw that up?"

"How could *they?* Hazel! You have to pay attention!" Rose yelled. "It's your fault, not theirs!"

"How did they even know where to send it?" I asked, screaming. I had a sneaking suspicion the people at Fire and Ice were out to get me, but I couldn't prove it—and it was ridiculous.

I heard music coming from down the hall and forced my gaze toward it. Three twenty-something men singing a bit off-key delivered the apology I'd scripted as they followed a maniacal-looking Ronin McKinsey directly toward me—one of whom was Tanner's brother. I had no idea he worked at Fire and Ice, but that answered my question. Tanner laughed his butt off, smacking his thighs as he bent over with laughter. Tee watched the entire thing unfold, shaking his head slightly. I knew what they were all thinking, but they were wrong. That wasn't what I wanted!

Ronin marched up to me, and the crowd surrounding us parted like the Red Sea. Perhaps I could explain the mistake before he broke up with me, then he'd see it wasn't my fault.

"I can explain, I swear."

"I hope so because I'm so mad right now, I..." He turned to face the three singing men. "Can you please shut up?"

They stopped singing, but they were still holding the melting cake while Ronin glared at them. Strawberry ice cream dripped onto the floor, making a huge mess in the hall that Principal Witt would probably make me clean.

"I... See, what happened was... I ordered a cake, but I clicked on the pick-up button, not the delivery button, see?" I handed him my phone, which was a mistake since I'd clearly done it wrong.

"It says you chose singing telegram, Hazel! A singing telegram!"

"But... No, see... right here, see how I clicked here? Well, I thought that was the option for pick-up, but it turns out they don't know how to design a website, so I actually clicked on... Well, that," I said as I pointed to the three men holding what now resembled a puddle of mud.

"Are you seriously trying to blame this on the website? Seriously? I told you to go home and figure out how to get the balloons down, not go home and order a singing telegram cake!" Ronin shouted, the little vein in his forehead pulsing so fast I worried it would rupture.

"But—"

"No, no buts, Hazel. I'm done. I can't deal with you anymore!" he said, accidentally backing into the men with the cake and toppling them all over. The four of them slipped in the melted ice cream and fell. Ronin landed square on top of the mud cake. He sat on the floor looking up at me with a murderous glare, half the school laughing at his butt stuck in an ice cream cake. Even the delivery men had to work to stifle a chuckle.

"Ronin, I... I'm really sorry, I was only trying to—"

"I don't care. I'm done. It's over. Have a nice life, you overbearing, control freak, smothering the life out of me, crazy person!" He stormed off, his pants covered with chocolate cake and ice cream. I stared after him, watching him turn the corner and out of my life completely.

I turned around to find my sister giving me the most sympathetic look she could muster. "I'll help you clean this up. Don't worry about it."

"Yeah," Dizzy said. "You're better off. He's a moron anyway." She waved off the entire monstrous ordeal like it was just another day in the life of a teenager, but it didn't stop the tears from falling. I tried not to cry in school, but the disaster, coupled with the broken heart, made it impossible.

The crowd started to dissipate. There were only two minutes until the late bell and the best of the action was already over. Principal Witt appeared with a stern look on her face. I nodded my head before she even spoke. "Yes, Ma'am, I know. I'll get right to it."

"Very well, and then you can come to see me in my office," she said, then walked back down the hall with purpose. I was in for a long lecture and maybe detention, fantastic.

"See, Hazel!" Sara yelled, and it surprised me. I'd all but forgotten she was there until she blew up out of nowhere. "I tried to tell you! All the time, I try and try, but you never listen to me. It's maddening!"

"Why are you screaming at her?" Dizzy asked. "Her boyfriend just broke up with her in a public place, and she already feels like crap."

"Well, how do you think I feel? I'm sick of constantly trying to stop her from doing stupid stuff, then I'm stuck picking up the pieces when it all goes wrong, exactly how I said it would. What do you think it does to my social status when I have a best friend who's an idiot?" she spat.

I flinched, never expecting those words to come from her mouth.

"You know what? Ronin got it right. I'm so sick of dealing with your crazy, over-the-top ways, Hazel. I support you, and all I get in return is embarrassment. We're done. This is over," Sara said.

"What? What's done? What's over?" I asked, thinking I misunderstood her.

"Us, our friendship. It's over, just like you and Ronin," she stated flatly, waving her hands like a crazy person.

"Are you serious right now?" Rose asked. "What kind of best friend are you?"

"The kind who knows when to cut her losses and get out while she still has some degree of dignity left. Have a nice life, Hazel." Sara stormed off to her next class, leaving me standing alone.

Alone... the boyfriendless, best friendless, solitary loser three weeks before prom.

"What just happened?" I asked Rose, who only took me in her arms and hugged me.

"Nothing important, Hazel. Forget those freaks. You don't need them," Dizzy said, feeling a lot more like a friend to me than Sara ever did.

The janitor dropped mops, a bucket of soapy water, and a trash can in the hall with a little sneer, then trudged off to do whatever it was he did when he wasn't cleaning up messes made by teenagers. The hall was empty except for the three of us, mopping up ice cream and chunks of cake. What a waste of good food. It occurred to me then I'd spent $75 to lose my boyfriend and my best friend in one fell swoop. I started to cry again, feeling alone and useless. Maybe they were right? Maybe there was something wrong with me that I hadn't seen?

I swiped the tears away before Rose and Dizzy saw. A soft grip squeezed my shoulder.

"Hey, don't cry," Tee said. "I came to check on you because... Well, that was... A-are you okay?"

I nodded because speaking would only make me cry more. He smiled and took the mop from me. "I'll help."

"Hey, Tee," Rose said, a slight blush forming on her cheeks. I didn't have time to worry about it or even make a mental note to ask her about it later. I was too lost in my own grief.

"Hey, Rose," Tee said, his eyes darting everywhere but toward my sister. After the proper amount of awkward silence, he turned his attention back to me. "Don't cry over Ronin, and especially not over Sara. She's an awful person. Everyone knows that. And Ronin, he's mad now, but I'm sure when he has time to think about it, he'll apologize, and maybe you can be friends?"

It was sweet that Tee tried so hard to cheer me up, but it would take more than a few kind words to heal the gaping wounds left by my ex-boyfriend and ex-best friend. "Cheer practice is going to suck now," I said.

"Nah. I'm sure the girls will stick up for you. Don't let Sara win. Don't give her what she wants," Tee said, alluding to the common knowledge that Sara had always wanted to be captain, and at one time thought she was more deserving of it than me—the one who designed all our cheers and tricks, the one who got us into the regional competition.

"Yeah, I'm sure you're right." I sighed and finished cleaning.

Little did I know Sara had already devised a plan to out me from my spot as captain, and it was one I never saw coming.

Three

- -

Rose and Dizzy gave me space to process everything that night, but the truth was, I probably could have used a few pep talks. Of course, I still had plenty of friends, but I'd lost my boyfriend and my best friend in a single day. Okay, so maybe Sara wasn't really a friend if she could walk away so easily, but it still hurt.

I couldn't sleep. I tossed and turned, worried about cheer practice and what games would be like watching Ronin. Prom was three weeks away, and not only was I single, but I seriously doubted any guy would want to go with me after witnessing the debacle in the hall with the ice cream cake. Before I realized it, my alarm went off, and I dragged my butt out of bed with zero sleep.

"Sit with us today?" Rose offered when she saw me enter the kitchen. Our parents were sitting at the table reading the newspaper while she filled bowls with cereal.

"Uh, maybe. I don't know. Maybe I'll eat alone," I mumbled, taking one of the bowls. Our mother's ears perked, but the great thing about Mom was that she never pushed. She knew

I'd confide in her when I was ready, and then she'd make it all better with chocolate chip cookies and shopping. That and advice which almost always involved shaking things off.

Dizzy showed up right on time. For whatever reason, I decided I'd ride to school with them instead of taking my own car. They talked about the usual things, occasionally including me in the conversation, but generally allowed me to sulk as I wished. I expected the day ahead to be a lot of things—humiliating, miserable, lonely, sad, heartbreaking, regretful—but in my wildest dreams, I never thought it would *also* be the day I'd walk into school to see my former best friend hanging all over my ex-boyfriend like a set of bad curtains.

"That dirty little... Grr," Dizzy said. "She planned it that way all along." Her eyes narrowed, homing in on Sara, and I'm sure Sara felt the chill. Sara shook off a shiver and went about tossing her hair over her shoulder in a dramatic display that showcased her ample, God-given goodies. Dizzy was a better friend than Sara ever was, and I was glad Rose was more than willing to share her best friend while I recovered from Sara's betrayal.

Ronin looked miserable, in physical pain every time Sara touched him, which gave me the slightest hint of satisfaction. I slammed my locker door closed, catching his attention. I gave him my best *I despise you* glare, which seemed to hit my intended target right in the gut. He looked sad, which sent a giddy shiver through me.

Sara was blabbering to Tanner's girlfriend about something, and all the while, Ronin stared at me. When Sara realized she was no longer the center of his attention, she pulled on his arm and led him down the hall. I had a sneaking suspicion my first-period class would be miserable, sitting there for an hour while Sara shot satisfied glances in my direction. Looks that said she had what she wanted, and I was the throwaway.

Ronin glanced over his shoulder as she dragged him along, helpless and sad. I chuckled, thinking of all the misery Sara would put him through, just like she had every boyfriend before him. "I'm pretty sure you're gonna miss me, Ronin McKinsey," I whispered.

"What?" Rose asked, adjusting the strap on her bag.

"Nothing. Let's just get this day over with."

We parted ways at the end of the hall, where I took a deep breath before turning the corner toward my first-period class with Sara. I stopped short when I saw her stand on her toes and kiss Ronin's cheek. That was bad enough, but before he could escape, she lifted herself again and kissed him smack on his lips.

It infuriated me. Not even one day. Not *one day* before Sara made her move, and not one day before Ronin forgot who I was and started kissing my ex-best friend. I was seething. If I followed her in that classroom, there was a good chance I would gouge her eyeballs out with my pencil. I already had detention for the cake incident. I suspected a second visit to Principal Witt's office, especially after physically assaulting another student, would land me a suspension at least. Maybe jail if I *did* gouge her eyeballs out. It felt worth it for a moment, then I came to my senses.

Even so, I couldn't do it. I couldn't face her, so I did the only thing a teenage girl whose awful best friend stole her boyfriend right out from under her could do. I reached up and pulled the fire alarm. I immediately hated myself. What was I thinking? Someone could get hurt in the dash to get outside, or worse.

Kids scrambled from classrooms, completely ignoring their teacher's pleas for organization and order. Ronin walked toward the exit, Sara hot on his heels. I followed not far behind. I had no idea where I was going, but I moved with purpose. I practically ran over some freshmen who got in my way and mumbled a quick apology I'm not sure they heard.

The crowd separated us, Ronin and Sara heading toward the practice field while my group was heading toward the main field. I darted toward the other group, narrowly avoiding getting caught and sent back by a teacher. The area filled quickly as kids flopped on the bleachers and started talking, grateful for the delay.

I saw no one I knew well enough to start a conversation with, so I stood there like a moron fiddling with the straps of my backpack. I slid it off and dropped it to the ground, planning to make a seat out of it, when I caught Ronin staring at me. His eyes remained focused on me, even as Sara talked his ears off. She'd make him look away soon, and I realized I had about a second to make him jealous before that happened.

I turned and grabbed the closest boy I could reach. "Kiss me!" I said, gripping his arm firmly.

"What?" he asked. His hazel eyes were pretty, and they distracted me momentarily from the task at hand.

"Kiss me, please," I said, glancing at Ronin, who looked very confused.

"Yeah, I'm not gonna kiss you, random person. Crazy, random, weird person I don't know." He tried to back away, but I had a firm grip on his shirt sleeve.

"I'll pay you," I offered, so desperate at that point, I didn't really care how I came across to the complete stranger I'd taken hostage.

"I'm not a prostitute," he said, causing me to release his shirt so I could slap my forehead with frustration. Why wouldn't he just kiss me? Was I that awful?

He started to back away and merge into the crowd when he looked at me again. He stopped, probably waiting to see what shenanigans I'd get myself into next. I sighed and sat on my bag, the moment lost. Ronin was talking to Tee, oblivious to me again. It was already hot outside, and I was regretting my move to pull the fire alarm as sweat slipped down my forehead. A shadow cast over me, and suddenly, I was lifted to a standing position.

It was the guy I'd asked to kiss me. His hand slid behind my neck, his fingers twisting in my hair until he had it completely wrapped up in his hands, a tangled mess. He pulled me forward, pressing his lips on mine in an almost, but not quite painful way. His kiss was warm and soft, and I forgot what I was supposed to be doing. Oh yeah, making Ronin jealous.

I slid my hands up his arms, settling them on his chest. He continued to kiss me, taking a chance that a teacher would see us and we'd both get in a heap of trouble. He didn't seem to care, and given how amazing the kiss was, I didn't care much myself.

He pulled back, leaving his hands in my hair. "He's raging with jealousy," he whispered in my ear.

"Huh? Who? What?"

"Ronin. You were trying to make him jealous, right?" I nodded, tangling my hair more in his hands.

"Mission accomplished." He wiggled his hands free and stepped away, turning to disappear back into the crowd. At the last second, he turned and closed the distance between us again. My hands draped around his neck as he lifted me slightly off the ground, holding me close enough so he could kiss me without getting a crick in his neck.

The bell rang, signaling the all-clear for us to go back to class. He released me, his hazel eyes a light shade of green in the sunlight.

"Now he's just fuming," he said, then left me to go to class, a puddle of Hazel Simmons standing in the practice field wondering what just happened. I touched my fingers to my lips, still a bit shocked and dazed while people flooded around me. Someone cleared her throat, and I glanced over my shoulder.

"Maybe this is none of my business, but why were you just kissing Daniel Starnes?" Dizzy broke my trance and unwittingly gave me the name of the mystery make-out boy.

"Daniel? Oh... I didn't know his name," I replied.

"You just kissed a random person you don't know?" she asked, urging me forward so I wouldn't be late getting back to class. "What has Ronin done to you?" she muttered under her breath, then said, "Maybe be careful with Daniel? No one really knows much about him. He's kind of a loner, and his sister was yanked out of school last year for who knows what reason."

"I'm not dating the guy, Diz. I just kissed him to make Ronin jealous." I waved her off, dismissing any thought of Daniel Starnes from my mind.

"That was a doozy of a revenge kiss, Hazel. From where I stood, it looked pretty intense." She opened the door that another student let slam in our faces because people had no manners. "He seems nice enough. I'm just saying be careful, that's all. Take from it what you will."

Luckily for me, first period was already over, so I wouldn't have to deal with Sara. However, second had only just begun when they let us back in, which meant I had six more hours of misery ahead of me, not counting lunch. I sighed and waved goodbye to Dizzy, glad I didn't have any other classes with Sara.

Turns out, I *did* have three classes with Daniel and had no idea. I sat in front. He sat in the back. I paid attention. He doodled all hour. I blushed when he walked by and smiled at me, which was evidently an invitation to sit closer to me. During our last class together, he sat directly behind me, making my stomach do weird things all hour.

I finished my work early and turned in my paper, catching Daniel staring at me as I did. I hoped I didn't make him think I was interested in him with the kiss. He was the first boy within reach when I was trying to make Ronin jealous. I hadn't thought much of the consequences, but then I guess I rarely did, exhibited by the balloons and singing telegram that sent my boyfriend packing in the first place.

I sat in my chair, trying to ignore the way Daniel's staring made me feel. Mostly because I didn't know what it was but also because he looked like he would devour me if given a chance. I counted the seconds until the class ended, the second hand of the clock moving way too slowly to be accurate.

When the bell finally did ring, I jumped from my seat and ran from the room. I was down the hall and out the door in a second, trailing down the front steps and toward Dizzy's car. I crossed the courtyard and hit the second set of steps, the last obstacle, before ending in the lot.

"Hey," Daniel said.

"Ahh!" I screamed, coming to a screeching halt. His voice in my ear surprised me. "How did you... H-how did you beat me to the parking lot?"

"Were we in a race? I didn't know, but I won. Cool." His russet hair was combed back out of his face, but a few locks managed to wiggle free and flop in the front, bouncing whenever he took a step. "So, listen, I was thinking—"

"Please don't ask me out. That thing earlier was dumb. I'm sorry, I just broke up with—"

"Ronin, yeah, yeah. I'm not asking you out. I want your help." He tugged my shirt sleeve, urging me through the lot. "I have a proposition for you."

We passed Dizzy's car, but neither she nor Rose was anywhere to be found. They probably weren't trying to avoid a boy they kissed during a false fire alarm, hence, no reason to rush. We stopped at the back of the lot, nowhere else to go, but no one around to hear us talking.

"What is it?" I asked.

"What is what?" he asked as he pulled his bag from his shoulder and dropped it to the ground.

"Your proposition?" I reminded.

"Oh, that. Yeah, I was thinking, if you can help me get a date for prom, I can help you get revenge on Ronin. Or make him jealous. Whatever it is you're trying to do," he offered, pulling a helmet from his bag.

"Okay."

"Okay, just like that?" he asked, pausing momentarily to make sure he heard correctly.

"Yeah. I'll do anything to get him back. It's a deal," I said, realizing a moment too late I might have made a deal with the devil himself.

"Huh. Well, I like a woman who knows what she wants. How do we do this, then?" he asked, preparing to slide the helmet over his head.

"How come I don't know anything about you? Where did you come from?" I asked aloud, though I'd intended to keep my inquiries to myself.

"Wow. I've been in the same classes as you all year. Nice to know how invisible I am. You must have a high opinion of me," Daniel said. He pulled the helmet on and clasped it under his chin. I wondered where he parked his bicycle since we'd already passed the bike racks long ago.

"Well, maybe if you joined activities or something, I'd know you existed," I said. Still, I felt a little bad that I had never noticed him.

He smiled and shook his head. "Whatever you say, Peaches. My house, right now. You can explain our French homework to me, then we can plan our attack."

"Your house?" I asked. "Yeah, I don't think so."

"Relax, my sister will be at home. We're not serial killers, Hazel." He knew my name. Okay, that wasn't weird. Of course, he did. Everyone did. But why did I *like* that he knew my name?

"Fine, I'll ask my friend to drop me off. What's the address?"

He slid the helmet back off and handed it to me. "No need. I can take you. Put this on."

I took the helmet, skeptical. "Uh, I don't think we'll both fit on your bicycle, Daniel. Also, what kind of bike helmet is this?" I stared at it, trying to figure out why the wind visor was necessary.

He glanced over his shoulder. "So, she does know my name. And who said anything about a bicycle? In what world does that look like a bicycle helmet to you?" He stopped beside a red and white motorcycle with the word Ducati painted on the side.

I handed him back the helmet. No way, not for me, thanks. There was no way I was getting on a motorcycle with some guy I just met. *But you did kiss him, Hazel,* my brain reminded me. He stood waiting for me to speak, but I had nothing. I made something up as fast as I could, so I wouldn't look like an idiot, but that ship had probably already sailed.

"Listen, I lost my boyfriend and my best friend in one day, then I got to watch my ex-best friend kiss all over my ex-boyfriend, so I'm a little stressed. I'll just get a ride and meet you there."

"Who cares about Sara? Best friends are overrated anyway. Look at me. I don't have any friends, and I'm awesome."

"You have friends. I saw you with them after the... the... the thing, you know," I said as my cheeks blushed. He chuckled at my inability to say the word kiss, but let it slide without comment.

"I have acquaintances. I do not have friends. There's a difference, but I'm glad you agree I'm awesome," he said.

"What? I didn't say that. When did I say you're awesome?"

"You didn't disagree when I said it. You said I have friends but didn't say I'm not awesome, ipso facto, you think I'm awesome."

"Ipso... what?" Daniel was confusing and wordy, not particularly concerned with what I thought of him or how his words made him appear. He slid onto his motorcycle and turned the key in the ignition, the bike roaring to life beside me. It all made sense then.

"Oh, I get it. So, you're a bad boy type," I said, proud to finally have him nailed down as a type. I could work with a type, but I could not work with ambiguity, which was what Daniel Starnes' personality had been until that point.

"I'm a say what now?" When he realized I wasn't getting on the bike just yet, he turned it off so he could hear me.

"A bad boy. You know, the motorcycle-riding, always getting into trouble, kissing random girls with a devil-may-care attitude, bad news, bad boy."

His eyebrows raised slowly, and his forehead creased. "Wow. You really put a lot of thought into that. You asked me to kiss you, by the way."

"Whatever, still a bad boy," I replied, trying to forget I offered him money to kiss me.

"I'm not that, whatever it is. Seriously, you really don't know me at all." He smirked, tapping his fingers on the handlebars of his bike.

"Say what you will, but I've pegged you, Daniel. You, sir, are a bona fide bad boy. Accept it. Deal with it. It's your high school tagline."

"You like cliché categories, don't you?"

"I was the head cheerleader dating the soccer captain. I'm a walking cliché category. That's what Sara always said, anyway," I said, dropping my head at the memory of my best friend ditching me after five good years together.

"Yeah, she's kinda right. She's still all sorts of words I should not say in public, but kinda right. Categorize away, Hazel, but one day you'll see not all of us fit in your little boxes. I don't care what anyone thinks of me. I do what I want when I want. What box does that go in?"

"Bad boy, Daniel. Textbook definition."

He smacked his forehead and ran his hands down his face. "Forget it. Put the helmet on before I rethink this whole partnership."

I slid the helmet over my head, my ponytail sliding down until it hung low at my neck. I glanced up at him as I adjusted the straps. "So, you really don't care what anyone thinks of you?"

"No, should I?" He steadied the bike, so I could climb on the back. It was the tiniest seat I'd ever seen, and my body slid forward until every inch of it was pressed against his. I tried to ignore that fact and responded.

"Yes! What if people think you're something you're not? You have to stay on top of your reputation, or people will think the wrong things about you," I informed him, trying and failing to put space between our bodies.

"Oh. My. Gosh. I can't believe it!" he said, throwing his head back.

"What? What's wrong?"

"I can't believe I've been doing high school all wrong! How did I survive before you, Peaches?" he asked, glancing over his shoulder.

"Not funny," I said. I slid down against him every time I tried to get back up on the tiny seat.

"You know what's not funny? How hard you are on yourself. How hard you try to fit this perfect image you think you're supposed to be. Stop caring, Hazel. Just stop caring and hold on tight."

With that, he released the brake, and I nearly fell from the bike. I wrapped my arms tightly around his waist and hung on for dear life. Daniel was right. He wasn't a bad boy at all. Daniel Starnes was a lunatic.

Four

"You are a terrible driver! You nearly killed me!" I shouted when Daniel pulled into the driveway of his home and parked his bike.

"I'd say I did well for someone who had a girl screaming in his ear every three seconds. Honestly, Hazel, your vocal cords are amazing," he said, taking the helmet I shoved in his face.

He opened the front door to a spacious living room filled with the scent of food. What, I had no idea, but it smelled divine. I followed him into the kitchen but never saw hide nor hair of this sister he claimed to have. He opened the oven, and the smell wafted over me.

"What is that? It smells fantastic," I said, breathing it in.

"I have no idea. My sister gets bored and cooks." He closed the oven and opened the fridge. "What do you like? Water? Juice?"

"Water's fine, thanks."

"Hungry?" he asked, but he didn't wait for my answer before piling snacks into my arms.

"How long are you keeping me here?" I asked, taking in the abnormally large pile of food he intended we eat during our planning session.

"Well, if you refuse to ride the bike again, I guess you're staying the night."

"Ha, ha, very funny," I said.

"He thinks so, but he's really just an annoying idiot." A beautiful blonde-haired girl appeared beside me, staring at Daniel with bright, expressive brown eyes. "The thing is, he's the only one who thinks he's funny," she whispered in my ear, sort of. Unlike Daniel, she was loud and invaded my personal bubble, but in all, she seemed like a nice person from what I gleaned in the two seconds she'd been in my presence.

"And this delightful pain in my butt is my sister, Rebecca," Daniel said, digging into a bag of potato chips.

"It's Becca, and you are?" She offered her hand. She stared past me and steadied herself with the counter.

"Uh... I'm Hazel. Hazel Simmons." I took her hand, and she shook it once, then released it. "It's so nice to meet you."

"Polite," Becca said, then she did the strangest thing. Her hands roamed my face, squishing my nose and poking at my eyes. She brushed her fingers over my lips and ended with her hands cupping my ears. "And really beautiful. Seriously, your face is super symmetrical. What color is your hair? It looks like a blob to me."

"It's brown, Becca. Can you stop before Hazel runs away screaming?" Daniel said, pulling me away and toward the stairs. "My sister is losing her vision. She has a degenerative disease that started affecting it about a year ago," he said, then yelled down the stairs. "Which is why she can't see when she's annoying the snot out of me!"

"I'm blind, Daniel, not deaf!" she yelled back. "I know I annoy you! I'm homeschooled. What else is there to do?"

He rolled his eyes and continued to drag me up the stairs toward his bedroom. At the end of the hall, he entered a room and flipped the switch. It was larger than mine and sparsely furnished, but it was neat and organized. So neat, it made me feel like my room was dirty, and I dusted it daily.

He flopped in a bean bag chair and pointed to the bed. "Take the bed. It's more comfortable."

I glanced at the bed, decided that was way too comfortable for a first meeting, sat on the floor across from him, cross-legged, and pulled out our French textbook. "I'm good on the floor, thanks. What part of the French work did you need help with?"

"All of it, starting with Bonjour," he said, offering me the chips.

"You mean to tell me you don't know any of it? It's been seven months, Daniel!" The fact that he didn't even know what hello was after seven months of class baffled me. "Are you even passing the class?"

"I don't know. Maybe?" He wiped his fingers on his pants and tossed the empty bag into the wastebasket.

"Daniel!"

"What?" he asked, mouth full of chips.

"How can you care so little about passing classes? It's our senior year! Don't you care about college?" I asked a little too excitedly.

"Of course not, he's already gotten into—"

"Becca! Go away!" Daniel shouted at his poor sister, who happened to walk by and interjected her thoughts. She looked so sad, I felt awful for her.

"Daniel, be nice to your sister."

"Yes, Mother," he said sarcastically, then said, "Becca, go away, *please.*"

Becca sighed and wandered away. Daniel stood from the bean bag chair and slammed his door closed. "I swear, I can't get one second of peace around here. And to answer your question, yes, I care, just not about French."

"Well, you still need to pass it, so you better start caring," I said and flipped back to the beginning of the book.

A door slammed downstairs, and voices drifted up to the bedroom. The house was large and an acoustic nightmare, which was why we heard every word of Becca's conversation with her friend, complete with the details of her new favorite lipstick color.

"This isn't gonna work," Daniel said, frustrated that we hadn't even made it past the first chapter in an hour, let alone discussed our plan to get him a date to prom and get Ronin back for me. "We need to find another place to hang out."

"We could go to my house, but Rose and Dizzy would probably drive you crazy, too," I said, realizing I hadn't bothered to tell either of them where I was or what I was doing. "I should probably call them."

"Call when we get there," he said, grabbing my hand and leading me out the door.

"My things," I said, trying to turn back as he dragged me through the house.

"I'm bored with French. We'll get them on the way back to your house. For now, we're going to find a better place to plot our revenge... I mean, whatever, you know what I mean."

"Not on that bike, we're not," I said, holding firm at the garage door.

"Chill, Peaches. We're taking my mom's car." He dangled the keys in front of me, and for some reason, I agreed. It was a little crazy, the idea of running around town with a boy I didn't really know, but Daniel was fun. He was a kind of fun I'd never experienced—carefree and happy-go-lucky.

"Fine, let's go." I climbed into the car, glad to have a roof and four sides on my transportation this go around. "Where are we going?"

"Not sure yet. We need to find a hangout where we can scheme and plot like devious little cheerleaders... I mean, devious little... Let's just find a place."

"Devious little cheerleaders?" I asked.

He shrugged. "Yeah, I said it. Sorry. But you have to admit—"

"Don't finish that sentence, or I will strangle you with my pompoms," I said.

His laugh was infectious, and I found myself wondering why he had trouble finding a date to prom at all. Surely, there was a girl in our school who was interested in him, I just had to find her—and fast.

Daniel parked downtown, dangerously close to a place I had no desire to see, let alone hang out inside. I hated it, but I doubted I'd ever walk into Fire and Ice again, not without Ronin beside me. I sighed and got out of the car and walked with Daniel, a pleasant stroll down the block—one I hoped would lead *away* from all those memories shared with Ronin.

"Where are we going?" I asked.

"You ask a lot of questions," he said. He glanced up and down the sidewalk, then turned left. "And I don't know. Let's just walk with no destination in mind and see where life takes us, Hazel."

Life had been beating me for two days, so I was less inclined to trust her opinion on where I should go. Nonetheless, I walked with him down the street to the row of shops I'd passed dozens of times on my way to get cake and ice cream.

When he approached Fire and Ice, I slowed. Surely, he wouldn't pick the one place in the entire town, I didn't want to go. Didn't he hear about the debacle with the ice cream cake? Daniel reached for the door, the familiar ding of the bell tingling in my ears.

"I can't eat here," I said, backing a few steps away.

"You can't, or you won't? Like you physically can't chew food here, or you'd rather eat dirt?" he asked, still holding the door.

I looked through the window, the corner booth taunting me. I wanted to puke. "Both, I think."

"Okay, why is that?" he asked.

Maybe he hadn't heard? Perhaps my humiliation was only known to the popular crowd who couldn't seem to stop talking about it. Or maybe, the more likely answer, Daniel simply did not listen to gossip.

"I just can't."

"But why? It's cake and ice cream. Cake, Hazel... and ice cream. Cake and ice cream. Together. In a bowl. A bowl full of yummy in the tummy happiness." He pointed at the shop and stared blankly at me, non-responsive as I watched people coming and going. How many times had Ronin and I kissed and cuddled in the corner booth?

"Cake and ice cream." Daniel flapped his hand in front of my face, jerking me back to reality.

"Because Ronin always brought me here after a game. It was our thing for over a year," I said, biting back the tears. He let the door close and dropped his hands to his sides.

"Oh," he whispered. "Um... maybe..." He glanced over his shoulder, then took a single step backward. He pulled open the glass door to the shop beside Fire and Ice, then motioned for me to enter.

"This is a dry cleaner, Daniel."

"Dry cleaning. It'll be our thing." He motioned for me to enter again as a blast of heat rushed from the little shop and flirted with my hair. It was already hot enough, so dry cleaners were a no-go. And who hung out in the lobby of a dry cleaner anyway?

"No," I said and shook my head.

"Fine." Daniel let the door shut and took several more steps backward, tugging at my shirt to pull me along with him. He opened the next door and motioned for me to enter.

"This is a flower shop, Daniel."

"Yeah. Flowers, our new thing."

I rolled my eyes and sighed, wondering how long this would go on, then shook my head.

"No? Geez, woman. You're hard to please." He took two more steps back and opened the last door on the block.

"This is a bookstore," I said.

He arched his eyebrows, and I nodded. It couldn't hurt to see what was inside. Besides, it had a little café, and I needed coffee. Copious amounts of coffee—enough to put me on a caffeine high so far up, I'd have too many tremors to worry about Ronin and Sara.

"Bookstore, it is then." Daniel ushered me in and opened his arms wide in the lobby, circled around, and shouted, "Welcome to your new thing Hazel Simmons. Books and that old sleeping guy over there."

He gained the attention of the woman at the check-out counter. She smiled a friendly hello and stuck her nose back in her book. I turned my head in the direction of Daniel's pointing finger and chuckled. "That's a giant stuffed bear in the kiddie corner, not an old man, Daniel."

He squinted. "Huh. So it is. Anyway, this here, this is us, Hazel. It's the Hazel and Daniel thing. Our hang out, our chill space, our hijinks headquarters, the—"

"Okay, I get it. What's your point?" I asked.

"The point is, you can do stuff without Ronin What's His Name."

"McKinsey, and I don't want to do things without him," I whined. "I don't like doing things without Ronin."

"I don't like the dentist, but I go because I'm a big boy, and I have to." I followed him toward the back of the store, row after row of books, many untouched and dusty.

"How is that anything like me not having a boyfriend to do things with?" I asked, leaning against the wall beside the shelf Daniel had stopped to peruse.

"I dunno. Maybe cuz my dentist sucks, just like your ex-boyfriend," he said matter-of-factly.

"That's not nice. You don't even know him."

"I know he's stupid." He looked over the shelf, up and down, seemingly searching for something.

"He's a straight-A student, Daniel. He's not stupid."

"I beg to differ. Differ has officially been begged." Daniel ran his fingers over a dusty shelf of mystery novels, then pulled one from the shelf and began flipping through it.

"Has anyone ever told you you're sort of an odd duck?" I asked, meaning no harm. I wondered if he'd always been that way or if it was for my benefit—his way of cheering me up and making me laugh by acting ridiculous.

He kept his eyes on the book. "Has anyone ever told you you're sort of... of... Anyway, Ronin is stupid."

"Okay. Tell me, why is Ronin stupid?"

Daniel slid the book back onto the shelf with painstaking slowness and lowered his gaze to meet mine. His hazel eyes shifted from one of curiosity and happiness to that of sorrow. "Because he broke your heart."

He pulled me closer and lifted me to his lips in one swift motion. His mouth settled onto mine haphazardly, but he found his place quickly and moved his lips slowly and purposefully. I melted again, goo in his arms, but unable to stop my thoughts from invading the wonderful feeling that spread over me.

What's happening? Why is he kissing me? Should I stop him? Do I want to stop him? Of course, I do. I love Ronin. Who's Ronin?

Daniel pulled back and looked toward the door just as it slammed shut. I peered through hazy eyes out the long window across the front of the shop, catching a glimpse of the boy I was desperate to get back at all costs. Ronin had seen everything. He was angry and stormed down the street like a child who didn't get his way.

Daniel smiled, his mission accomplished. "Jealous, jealous," he said.

Daniel made his way toward the café, again leaving me a puddle on the floor. He knew Ronin was at Fire and Ice. He knew Ronin would see us and, perhaps, follow us. I knew then, I was dealing with a mastermind, already working the plan before I even knew I was a part of it.

Five

D aniel's eccentric personality was difficult to get used to, but it was also unusually endearing—kind of like owning a chihuahua. You never knew what they would do, but they were sort of cute in their own way.

After the Ronin incident in the bookstore, I couldn't stop my mind from wandering. Did Daniel really know Ronin would be there, or was it a giant cosmic coincidence? And if he did, why didn't he bother to tell me our plan was a go? *We need a name for the plan... focus Hazel.* Furthermore, what was Ronin doing at Fire and Ice? Did he take Sara there?

I couldn't focus on anything, so I made a silly excuse to leave. Daniel took me home after collecting my things from his house. He knew I was lying when I said I had laundry to do, but I appreciated that he didn't call me on it. I'd have to find a really amazing girl for him to take to prom, one who would be a good potential girlfriend as well. She'd have to be open-minded for sure because if there was one thing Daniel Starnes was most definitely not, it was normal.

I dodged Rose and Dizzy in the kitchen, grabbed a drink, and mumbled a hello before making my way to my bedroom to ponder the possibilities for Daniel. Maybe Gina Brooks? She seemed nice, and she did her own thing, sort of like him. Or even, dare I say, Dizzy Martin? She had a mind of her own, a lot like Daniel. I sighed, coming up with no one else off the top of my head.

Now, what to do about Ronin? He was clearly upset when he caught Daniel kissing me, but was it because he missed me or because he was still mad at me? I thought about it until I fell asleep well after midnight. I wish I'd gotten more sleep because if I had, I might not have been such a crybaby the next day.

It started out okay. The first period with Sara wasn't so bad, especially since I snagged a seat in the back and ignored her hair-flipping all period. She was all over Ronin between classes, which was irritating, but what could I do about it without making myself a bigger target for ridicule? I'd humiliated myself enough for one week, thank you.

After the second period, strange things started happening. Ashley ignored me when I called her name, and she sped up so I couldn't catch her. Miriam told me she was too busy to go over the physics homework with me, which we did every single day. Then, more surprising than any of the other slights, sweet Erin, who never said a mean word to anyone, snapped at me when I asked to borrow a pencil during fourth period. I had no idea what was going on, but it sucked. However, it was lunch that did me in. I swapped out my morning books for my afternoon books at my locker and grabbed my lunch, ready to sit down and take a break from all the strangeness. But when I got to my regular table, the cheer squad table with the rest of the cheerleaders, someone was in my seat... Sara.

"Oh, hi, Hazel," Brit said with a guilty tone. "Um, I think we need to talk."

"Okay," I said cautiously. I tried to put my lunch down, but Ashley pushed it away. "What's going on?" I knew Sara and I were on the outs, but I assumed the girls wouldn't choose sides. I thought wrong.

"It's nothing personal, Hazel, but we decided we want Sara to be captain. We voted, and it's been settled," Ashley said.

"I'm sorry, we who? Who told you, you could have a random vote and out me with no discussion?" I asked.

"The handbook, page twenty-one, paragraph four," Sara said. Her sickly sweet and falsely sympathetic voice made me want to jump the table and stab her with her fork.

"And you all decided this?" I asked, giving Erin a good stare-down.

"It's just... with all your drama, and—" Erin started, but I wasn't having it.

"I got you to regionals! I did with my cheers. Mine, not Sara's, mine. And this is how you repay me?" I yelled, garnering more attention than necessary and likely hammering the final nail in my social status' coffin.

"Well, yeah, you did all that, but we think you're in a bad place right now. We're concerned that cheering will come second to... to... Well, frankly, second to the drama that surrounds your life," Miriam said.

I looked at Sara, who had a satisfied smirk on her face. I'd always known she was rough around the edges, but I never thought she was a knife-wielding psychopath who pounced the moment her so-called friend's back was turned. I felt that knife twisting in my back as a bone-chilling tingle surged down my spine.

I growled—a rumble that started in the pit of my stomach and rose through my chest until it erupted into something resembling a howler monkey on a sugar high. I was positioned to pounce, but a strong arm wrapped around my waist and stopped me from doing something stupid like attacking Sara in the middle of the cafeteria.

"Peaches, why are you trying to sit at the loser table?" Daniel asked—his laid-back attitude a stark contrast to the crazed monkey he held back. He leaned forward and whispered in my ear, "Easy, they aren't worth the time."

"Huh?" I managed to ask, unsure what was happening in my blind rage.

"Come, sit with me." Daniel picked up my lunch and slid his hand into mine. He gave the girls a long once over, one at a time, with a disgusted look on his face. "You're too pretty for this table."

The speed at which their jaws dropped made me plenty happy, and I forgot I wanted to rip Sara's eyeballs out. Everyone in the cafeteria stared at us, watching the former cheer captain and ex-girlfriend of *the* Ronin McKinsey follow a guy they didn't know existed... until we stopped at... the stoner table.

"What are you doing?" I asked in a hushed tone, not wanting to offend anyone but also not all that excited about sitting with a bunch of potheads.

"Sitting at the stoner table, why?" Daniel slid into a chair, but there was nowhere for me to sit. The table was full, so I stood there like an idiot. Not that they noticed since they were all too high to even see straight. They were all perfectly nice people, but I just wasn't into... whatever they regularly did.

I bent over and whispered in Daniel's ear, "But... you're not a... you don't do stuff, right?"

"No. Why does it matter?" he asked, gazing at me expectantly.

"But—"

"Peaches, Peaches, Peaches... That's what I keep trying to tell you. If you don't categorize yourself, then you get to do whatever you want. I'm in a quiet mood, so I sit with the quiet people who don't judge me. Now, sit and enjoy your lunch in silence." He scooted over in his seat and pulled me down beside him, then handed me half a sandwich.

The gasp in the cafeteria forced a blush on my cheeks. I looked up to see half the room still staring at us—including Ronin. He was baffled, but his confusion quickly morphed into something else. His eyes narrowed, lips pursed until they were nearly white, fists clenched at his sides.

"Don't look now, Peaches, but I'd say someone is good and jealous," Daniel said, inspecting my lunch bag for anything good.

"How do you seem to know exactly when he's watching and exactly what to do to tick him off?" I asked.

"I'm observant, and he's always watching you. I don't get it, really. Why'd he break up with you in the first place?" Daniel asked, arching his eyebrows as he held my apple. I waved him off, not hungry enough to fight for the apple. He bit into it and wrapped his arm tightly around my waist. It should have been uncomfortable since I barely knew him, but it was kind of cozy.

"Aren't you that girl that filled the gym with balloons?" A boy I didn't know stared at me with a cheesy smile.

"Jeff, you're high as crap. How are you functioning right now?" Daniel asked. Jeff started laughing so hard that he fell off his chair. I giggled, which got the rest of the table laughing.

"And this, folks, is why we don't do drugs," Daniel said, rolling his eyes.

Once I stopped giggling long enough to speak, I answered Daniel's question. "It was that, actually, the balloon thing followed by the accidental singing telegram and cake delivery."

Daniel blinked at me, staring into my eyes for an inordinate amount of time before responding. "And?"

"And that's it. Ronin says I'm too over-the-top for him. I guess I embarrass him or something." I *knew* I embarrassed him. I just never knew how much until he was screaming at me in the hallway after the cake debacle.

"And?" Daniel asked.

"And? I told you, I embarrass him with the things I do. The balloons, the cake, that time I sent him a dozen roses on Valentine's day, the huge posters on game day, the—"

"Whoa, whoa, whoa. You're saying he dumped you because you do nice things for him?" Daniel and half of the table waited for my answer.

"Well, I meant for them to be nice, but—"

"What?" Jeff asked, barely hanging onto his seat. "I wouldn't dump a girl for being nice." He smiled. A sweet smile, but his eyes were bloodshot and wandered all over my body.

"Thank you for your assessment, Jeff. Now, if you'd kindly butt out of my conversation with Peaches, I'd appreciate it," Daniel said, standing with me.

"He's just trying to be nice, Daniel."

"He's hitting on you, Peaches." Daniel led me out of the cafeteria and into the courtyard, where we could talk alone. "Don't date stoners, Peaches. They're worse than Ronin."

"I had no plans to date him. I'm trying to get Ronin back, remember?" I said, sitting on one of the benches that had been purchased by money raised in a cheer fundraiser I single-handedly put together. I wanted to go back inside and strangle Sara, but something told me Daniel wouldn't allow it.

"Right, that. Well, what do you hope to accomplish with this plan, Peaches? Keep making him mad until he caves and takes you back, or something else?"

"I need to find a way to make him so jealous he can't stand it, then he'll remember what it was like without me. And, maybe pull back a little after we get back together," I said.

"Pull back? Pull back what?" he asked, sitting on the ground in front of me.

"Pull back. You know, be a little less pushy and overbearing, less over-the-top. A little less me and a little more like the kind of girlfriend he's looking for," I said.

"So, you want to change yourself for him?" He slid closer and turned around, leaning his back against my legs. People were watching, and I assumed that was the effect he was going for. If we were the talk of the school, it would surely tick Ronin off.

"Precisely. Just a few adjustments, that's all."

"Why would you do that?" he asked, fiddling with my shoelaces.

"Because I love him, and sometimes you make adjustments for the people you love."

"I think your logic is flawed, Peaches," he said, tilting his head back to look me in the face.

"How so?"

He lowered his head and mumbled, "Shouldn't he love you the way you are?"

His question caught me off-guard, and it hit a place inside of me that made me realize he might be right, but Ronin was worth it. Ronin McKinsey was undoubtedly worth changing for. "Sure, but... but, just... Are you gonna help me or not?"

He shrugged, still playing with my shoelaces and staring at the ground. "Sure, whatever you want, Peaches, as long as I get a date to prom."

That name again, for the thousandth time. "Why do you call me Peaches?"

"You don't like it? I could call you Petunia, or Short Stack, or Half-pint, or Chicken Wing..." he rattled on.

"Why would you call me Chicken Wing?" I asked, regretting the question the moment it passed my lips.

"Dunno, maybe you like it better than Peaches?" He tilted his head back again to gauge my reaction, his hazel eyes a more golden-brown than green thanks to his shirt. Funny, how the eyes shifted color from golden to green. If only I, Hazel Simmons, could change as easily as hazel eyes.

"Why don't you call me Hazel?" I asked.

"Why would I?"

"Because it's my name, and that's what everyone calls me."

"I'm not everyone, Chicken Wing." His head in my lap was distracting. I almost forgot we were supposed to be plotting and scheming like devious little cheerleaders, a comment I wholeheartedly agreed with after the lunch incident.

"You're not everyone? Who are you then?" I asked.

"I'm Daniel. I thought we established that on day one." How he managed to keep a straight face when he said stupid stuff was beyond me.

"You're infuriating. Did you know that?"

"I'm inwhatiating?"

"Infuriating. Maddening. Impossibly annoying. Don't you pay attention in English class either?" I asked.

"No, not really. I grew up speaking English, so I figure I'm good." I resisted the urge to brush the hair away from his forehead, the locks that kept falling from the part he combed.

"What *do* you pay attention to, Daniel?"

He lifted his head, checking his wrist for an imaginary watch. "Hmmm... Hey, look at the time. Better get to class before the late bell, Chicken Wing." He leaped up, gathered his things, and started to walk away, something he always seemed to do—walk away when the moment was all wrong for walking away. I suppose it was something I'd just have to get used to.

"Daniel?" I called after him.

"Hmm?" he hummed, stopping a few feet away.

"Call me Peaches."

He smiled his crooked smile and waved, then disappeared into the crowd of students heading toward fifth period. All the while, Hazel Simmons melted into a puddle of goo thanks to a pair of hazel eyes and a crooked smile. *What is happening to me?*

It took all of fifth and half of sixth period for me to think of something besides Daniel, namely my plan to get Ronin back. If I could just sit him down and explain, he'd know the cake thing was an accident and it was meant to be private. Of course, that wouldn't change the dozens of other things I'd done that were too much for him. What I couldn't understand was what had changed. Ronin and I had been friends for three years before we started dating. He knew me. He knew what I was about and the way I showed people I loved them. What did he expect would happen once we started dating?

I felt a tap on my shoulder, distracting me from useless thoughts. I looked over my shoulder, and Brian Vargas shoved a note in my face. I took it, wondering what he had to say to me.

Rose is upset. She's worried about you.

I glanced back over my shoulder to find Dizzy staring at me from her seat in the corner. I had no desire to pen an explanation that would be passed through half a dozen hands before reaching her, so I nodded, hoping she got the clue.

She didn't. Brian tapped my shoulder again and passed me another note.

Crotch-rocket boy has been pacing in the hall for ten minutes.

I looked up to find Daniel peering into the classroom. When he caught my attention, he motioned for me to come out. I didn't know what he expected me to do. It's not like I could just get up and walk out of class. Brian tapped my shoulder again, then offered a frown and a sigh.

"Sorry," I whispered as I took the note.

Get a hall pass, doofus.

My hand shot up before I could stop it. "Yes, Miss Simmons?" Mr. Adams asked.

"May I have a hall pass, please?"

"For?"

"Uh... um..." Daniel danced around outside, clutching his stomach. "Oh, my stomach. I feel sick."

"Of course. Take a homework sheet on your way out, please."

I gathered my stuff, swiped a sheet from the top of the stack, and met Daniel in the hall.

"What is your problem?" I whispered, dragging him out of the teacher's line of sight.

"I got bored," Daniel said. "Let's skip seventh and go to the bookstore."

"You... Are you... You..." I was simmering, ready to blow up at the irresponsible boy. "Calculus is my worst class, numbskull! I need to pay attention in that class, but instead, I'm standing out here looking at a... a..."

"Numbskull? So, the bookstore then?" he asked.

"No! I'm going back to class where you should also go, Daniel. I'll meet you there after school." I started to walk away, but he grabbed my wrist and spun me around to face him.

"Skip this one class with me, and I'll tutor you in calculus. Easiest A of your life, Peaches."

"Right, and pigs fly over the ocean." I scoffed.

"Your loss, but you should know..." he started but didn't finish. His gaze trailed on something behind me. When I started to turn around, he stopped me. I wiggled free from his grip. "Hazel—"

"What is it? What's your problem?"

"I'm... I'm sorry," he said, then let me turn around.

There, down the hall, was Ronin McKinsey kissing someone who was not me. It also wasn't Sara. I couldn't see who she was, but it made my heart drop all the same. My heart was in grave danger of falling to pieces, and it demanded immediate attention. Well, if Ronin could suck someone's tonsils out in the hall, so could I!

I grasped Daniel's shirt collar and pulled the colossal boy down to my height before kissing him. I made a big deal out of *accidentally* kicking the lockers to ensure Ronin noticed. He did, but it didn't have the effect I was looking for. When I released Daniel, I saw Ronin shake his head, then grasp the girl's hand before he turned the corner. My heart dropped.

"Let's get out of here," Daniel said. He took my hand and led me out the double doors toward the parking lot. "Are you okay?" he asked.

"No. I'm not. That was too convenient like he planned it just to hurt me." I didn't want to cry in front of Daniel but cry I did.

"How is that possible, Peaches? He couldn't have known you'd come out of the classroom. It was a freaky coincidence, that's all. Don't cry over this." Daniel pulled me into a hug, one that I got lost in. I hadn't paid much attention to it before the hallway kiss, but he towered over me. I felt smaller than ever, a short little basket case who was using someone to make her ex jealous.

"I'm sorry, Daniel. I keep using you to get back at him. It's not fair." I shoved my face into the crook of his shoulder, which was better than letting anyone else see me cry.

"Hey, I'm holding you to the prom date thing, don't worry. Besides, it's not like kissing you is total torture or anything," he said.

"No?" I asked, suddenly feeling much better. *How'd he do that?*

"Nah, it's only partial torture." I shoved him, and he stumbled a few feet before laughing and coming back to me. "Come on, let's get some coffee and bother that sleeping old man at the bookstore."

"I told you, it's a giant teddy bear."

"So, you said, but we never did go inspect it to be sure. He could still be there, Peaches, just waiting for someone to wake him up and send him on his way. Wouldn't you feel awful knowing you were that person and you didn't do your civic duty?"

I laughed again, feeling so much better. "Daniel?"

"Yep?"

"Thanks."

"Anytime, Peaches. Anytime."

I adjusted my bag with a new determination. I'd find Daniel the best prom date imaginable, and I'd make Ronin squirm as much as possible while I worked my plan. Besides, there was some satisfaction in knowing Sara didn't win.

"What about Gina Brooks?" I asked.

"What about her?" Daniel asked. I noticed we were holding hands as we walked through the parking lot, but it was okay. I didn't mind it.

"As a prom date?"

He stopped short, nearly jerking my arm from its socket. "Are you serious?"

"Yeah, why not? She's pretty and funny, and a free spirit, just like you. I think you'd really like her," I said, trying to convince him to give her a chance.

"You're right. I do really like Gina. She's great, but I have this thing," he said, a smirk on his lips.

"A thing? What, you don't like redheads?" I asked. "Cuz it's a bit hypocritical of you."

"I like them just fine, but I do have a serious aversion to taking my own cousin to prom, Peaches." He chuckled and shook his head. "You really don't know anything about me, do you?"

I didn't, and as I stood there watching him smile back at me, I realized I wanted to. *How strange.* There was this boy who I didn't even know existed, and, for whatever reason, he was in the right place at the right time. And now, I almost couldn't imagine what life would be like without Daniel and his crazy ways.

Six

After convincing Daniel to walk instead of daring his deathtrap of a bike, he rambled on about anything and everything that popped into his mind, including the fact that we never did check to make sure the stuffed bear was not a sleeping old man. The moment we arrived at the bookstore, I made a beeline toward the children's reading corner.

"See, I told you. It's an abnormally large teddy bear, Daniel," I said, handing him the bear that was almost as tall as me.

"You can't be sure, Peaches." He took the bear and studied it, then turned it to face me, clutching it to his chest. "There could be a tiny old man in there just begging to be rescued from the monotony of listening to Curious George every day of his life."

"You're an odd duck, Daniel. A very odd duck."

"So, you mentioned both yesterday and again today. What's your deal with ducks? Did ducks scare you to death in a former life?" He dropped the bear back onto the tiny chair it called home, its button eyes looking up at me. I shivered, thinking of a little man stuck inside of it.

"It's a saying, Daniel. It's just something people say when they meet someone unusual. No, I did not die at the hands of fiendish feathery fowl in a former life. Your brain is just... You're just crazy." We walked toward the tiny café to study and plot. I needed coffee if I was to be alert enough to understand anything Daniel was trying to say.

"A fiendish... *what?*" He shook his head, confused.

"A fiendish feathery fowl in a former life. Say that five times fast," I teased.

"I can't even say it once at a normal pace, Peaches. So, is this our thing? Is this the thing we do now?"

"We've been friends for all of two days. How can we possibly have a thing?" I asked.

"You can have a thing in two days. You can have a thing in two minutes. A thing is a thing, and if a thing is working, then you don't question it. You accept it. This is our thing." He pulled out a chair for me, then dropped his backpack into the seat beside me.

"What exactly is our thing, then? Being devious?"

He rolled his eyes. "No, Peaches. Banter. Banter is our thing. And this teeny tiny little bookstore with an old man stuck in a bear is our place." The bear, *again* with the bear.

"Banter in a bookstore with bears?"

"What's your deal with tongue twisters and ducks? Ducks and tongue twisters, is that some crazy thing you do all the time? It's totally cool if it is. I just need to know so I can make some adjustments," he said.

"Adjustments for what? Why would you need to make adjustments?"

"Because you're my friend, Peaches. And we adjust for the people we care about," he said as he settled across from me and leaned close.

"I don't get it."

"I think I need to adjust, change a bit. I'm not good at tongue twisters, and I kind of hate ducks. That's two things that I obviously need to change about myself if we are ever going to be great friends. I don't really want to change, but I will if I have to."

"Why would you change anything about yourself just to be my friend? That's the stupidest thing I've ever heard anyone say," I replied, wondering why he was so dramatic over ducks and tongue twisters.

"And thank you for proving my point. Well done, Hazel Simmons. You now understand the fact that you should not have to change for anyone to like you." He sat back with a satisfied grin, almost taunting.

"Okay, thank you for making me feel like a moron while you made your point," I said, dropping my books on the table with an angry thud. I had already been humiliated enough for one lifetime, let alone a few days. "I don't need a guy to point out every stupid thing about me, thanks."

He popped straight with a sorrowful expression. "I'm sorry. That wasn't my intention, Peaches, but it is kind of silly to think that changing things about yourself will make Ronin happy. If he doesn't like you how you are, then that's his problem, not yours," he said, his tone instantly shifting from triumphant to sympathetic. "I just... Look, you *know* you are amazing. You're right. You don't need some guy to tell you that, but maybe you need a *friend* to remind you when you seem to forget. I'm trying to be that friend, even if the way I went about it was sort of... *jerky.*"

I sighed and dropped my head onto the table. I hadn't meant to make him feel bad just as much as he hadn't meant to hurt me.

"I think maybe *change* is too strong a word. I think I just need to, I don't know, not go so overboard, I guess." I tried and failed to describe what I felt. I loved grand gestures—the thoughtfulness, the planning, and the looks on the faces of my loved ones when they received said gesture. It all made me happy. But what good were they if they pushed away the people I cared for most?

"I still don't understand what it is you did wrong." Daniel shifted and tugged on my elbow. I groaned and sat up.

"I embarrassed him. I embarrass him all the time. I pull these big stunts to show him how I feel about him, and I guess all this time, they've really bothered him. And let's not forget the fact that those huge stunts end up going way off track." I flipped through my book, trying to avoid Daniel's intense gaze. It was green ten minutes before we sat but shifted to more of a greenish-gold under the café lighting. They really were beautiful.

He shrugged. "So, you filled the gym with a few hundred balloons. What's the big deal? I still don't get it."

"It was more than three thousand balloons, Daniel. Even I'm starting to understand why that was a bad idea."

He pulled his own books from his bag and dropped them dramatically on the table. I didn't know if he was mimicking me or if he was agitated, but the lady behind the counter gave him a glare. *Shut up or get out*—it said.

"You know what? Ronin is an idiot. I would love it if someone filled a huge gym with balloons for me because they thought it would make me happy." Daniel was frustrated, but who knew why?

"I think it's safe to say you and Ronin are nothing alike."

"Thanks, I'm glad you think so," he said with a smirk.

"You know what I mean. You're... He's... You're... You're just very different people." I sighed and tapped my pencil on my calculus book, hoping the answers would somehow fall out of the pencil and onto my paper.

"You say that like it's a bad thing. I'm glad I'm not an idiot who broke your heart because you did something nice for me. In fact, I pride myself on being the complete and total opposite of Ronin McKinsey in every way," Daniel said.

I looked up from my work, doubtful. "So, you're telling me if you walked into the gym and found it covered with balloons and all your closest friends teased you about it, it wouldn't make you a little upset? Oh, and don't forget the singing telegram cake you then fall into in front of half the school. It would have no impact on you whatsoever?"

"Of course, it would," he said.

"See, I told you. It was too much, and I am beginning to understand that. All I want to do is find ways to show him I appreciate him that don't embarrass him—or me, in retrospect," I argued.

"I meant, of course, it would, but not the same way it did him because, like you so aptly put it, we are nothing alike."

I sighed, growing tired of talking about it. "Fine, Daniel, how would you react if I'd done that to you?"

"Oh, look at the time. We better get to work on that French homework if we're going to get it finished before the store closes," Daniel said as he opened his French book to where we'd left off the day before.

"You're avoiding the topic, Daniel. Why is that?" *Got him.* He knew he'd react the same way, and he was trying to get out of the situation.

"Because I'm bored with it. That, and it's time to figure out who I'm going to ask to prom." He changed the subject again.

"I thought you said we needed to study the French homework?"

"Fine, teach me how to ask someone to prom in French," he said sarcastically.

"No, first calculus because you promised."

"Fair enough. What are you studying in calculus?" he asked, looking over my shoulder.

"I have no idea. I missed the class, remember?"

"Why'd you miss the... Oh yeah, that was me. Ha-ha, oops." Daniel's stupid grin actually made him look adorable, but I was too annoyed with him to care. I wished I could be as careless and free as he was, but then I probably wouldn't get into a decent college if I were.

I rolled my eyes, doubting he could help me at all. "All I have is this homework sheet that I don't know how to do because you dragged me out of class for this, Daniel. For old men stuck in bears and duck tongue twisters. I'm going to fail this miserable class," I groaned.

"You're not going to fail calculus, Peaches," he said, mocking me with a groan of his own.

"I will if I don't figure this crap out. It's impossible, and when will I ever need it?"

He blinked at me. "Like, you literally do math every day of your life, woman. Here, give it to me. I'll do it for you so you'll get a good grade, then I can start tutoring you tomorrow... right after you help me with French... and English Literature." He took the sheet and glanced over it.

"You already know how to do it?"

He looked up at me and chewed on the inside of his cheek. He struggled with something, and it was obviously more than whether he knew how to do the work or not. Somehow, I managed to stop the incessant flow of nonsense that normally spilled from his lips. Frankly, it made me sad. I didn't like seeing him concerned, especially when I didn't know the reason. It was a complete one-eighty in a split-second.

"What is it? Did I do something wrong?" I asked.

"Of course not. I, uh, I've already taken Calculus, so I should remember this."

He decided. He'd chosen his path. He lied to me. He was a bad liar, but I didn't think we were anywhere near close enough to question why he chose to lie. I also couldn't figure out how the truth could be so awful he *needed* to lie. Even so, I was horrible at letting things drop, so I pried a little.

"Oh, when did you take it?"

"Uh... last year. Right, last year... I think." He was already working on the problems, his pencil moving along the notebook paper at lightning speed. When he noticed I was watching, he slowed down and erased something. Then altered the rate at which he completed the problems, still faster than I'd ever be able to complete one, let alone a dozen... and he never touched the calculator, not even to turn it on.

"Last year? So, what are you taking now? AP Calculus? Honors?" I asked, impressed.

"Sure," he mumbled. He shut me out, a bizarre thing since he had no issue with delving into *my* life head-first. The pencil flew across the sheet at lightning speed again with little pause to even read the sheet. He couldn't seem to help himself; he just couldn't slow down, even if it was to trick me into believing he struggled with the problems. *Why? Why would he do that?*

Every few minutes, he'd notice I still watched him and would slow down, but when I looked away, he went right back to flying through it.

"So, who do you have for AP?" I asked.

"Morrison," he mumbled again.

I smacked my hand on top of his, breaking his concentration. "Why are you lying to me?"

He stared at me blankly, then slowly parted his lips and dropped his gaze back to the page. "Um... Do I have to talk about it?"

He looked so sad, so unlike Daniel Starnes in every way. All I wanted to do was reach across the table and hug him. I'd spent so much time worrying about how I would get Ronin back I'd forgotten, yet again, that I didn't know all that much about my new friend and partner in crime.

"No, not if you don't want to. But if you ever do, I'm here to listen," I said, taking my homework sheet away from him so I could look it over. "You know, I do need to learn how to do this, so maybe you can explain as you go?"

He scratched his head, ruffling up his hair more than it already was. "Yeah, right. So, the first problem is pretty easy."

"Not for me. It makes no sense how there are so many right answers. How do you get a range like that?" I asked.

"You can't look at this like you do other math. It's not as simple as solving for x, or two plus two. It's a study of continuous change, and change doesn't stay the same by definition. That said, your answer will most usually be... What's the matter, Peaches?" he asked when he glanced up at me.

I blinked at him several times. "You lost me at solve for x."

He smiled his crooked smile and dropped his head to the table. When he lifted it, old Daniel was back. "Okay, open your book, and let's do this."

I did as he asked and opened my book to the day's lesson, which looked like a bowl of alphabet soup mixed with a lot of symbols. How is it even math when it's mostly letters and symbols?

"You look sick. Are you gonna puke on me?" Daniel asked, leaning back in his chair.

"No, don't be silly. I'm just... This is really intimidating to me. Give me Austen or Dickens or Shakespeare, and I can pick it to bits, line by line, and tell you every thought and emotion and underlying message in every one of their works, but this... This is Greek to me."

"Well... It kind of is. Calculus comes from the Greek word—"

"Okay, who are you?" I demanded. "Because you're not the same person I walked in here with, Daniel. If you don't want to explain, that's fine, but you should know you're kinda freakin' me out!"

His jaw dropped, and the cranky counter lady shushed us. He glanced around, and even though the café was empty except for the counter lady and us, he still felt it necessary to drag me by the wrist to the back of the store and into the darkest, most remote corner he could find.

"You promise me right now, Hazel Simmons, if I tell you the truth, you take it to your grave."

"Don't be so dramatic; it can't be that big a deal," I said as he pulled me to the floor. I sat across from him, cross-legged as usual.

"I'm a genius," he said.

I shook my head. "I thought you were going to tell me something serious, Daniel. You're such a doofus," I said.

He cleared his throat. "Um... I actually mean that. I have genius-level IQ."

"Would you stop it and teach me how to..." I paused to study his face, and when I found no signs of jest, my jaw dropped. I couldn't stop my eyes from bulging when it finally hit me. "You're serious? You're a freaking genius! Like a real genius!" I yelled.

He clamped his hand over my mouth. "I said, take it to the grave, Peaches, not wake the dead announcing it to the world."

"But why?" I mumbled against his hand. He removed it and wiped my spit on his pants. "Why, Daniel? It's a good thing. And why on earth are you going to regular high school?"

"I don't want people to think I'm weird, okay?"

I giggled. "I'm pretty sure that ship has sailed, Daniel."

"You know what I mean. People will hound me for tutoring and other crap. I don't like people, Peaches," he said, seeming genuinely miserable at the idea of people approaching him about anything, let alone tutoring.

"But... but you like me, right? We're friends, I thought."

He scoffed. "You're not people, Peaches. You're Peaches. Of course, I like you."

"Okay, so what's the big deal then? Your secret is safe with me."

Daniel sighed and relaxed against the bookshelf. "Good. That's good. Thank you."

"I'm curious, though, where are you going to college? I'd bet—"

"I'm not," he said, his body tense again.

"Not what? Not sure, or not going?"

"Not going. I mean, not right after high school, anyway."

I blinked at him again, feeling like I was looking at a space alien. Why wouldn't he go to college? "I'm sorry. What do you mean you're not going?" I asked.

He sighed. "Because I don't need to, Peaches. I already have a job after graduation."

"I think you can do better than an entry-level job, Daniel. You're a freaking genius."

"I never said it was entry-level. I'm not sweeping floors at a fast-food chain, Peaches. I'm..." He hesitated, debating again.

"Daniel, I'll never say a word to anyone about your life, I promise. I wouldn't do that to you."

"Why not?" he asked, his voice surprisingly husky and weighted with worry that I could betray his most deeply held secret.

"Because I trust you, and that means something to me. Trust is a big thing in my family, and I value it very much. I will do everything in my power to return the favor," I said, placing my hand on his knee. He flinched slightly, so I thought I'd overstepped by touching him. I jerked my hand back and dropped them into my lap.

He pulled his legs up to his chest and rested his arms on his knees. The move essentially blocked my view of him, so I slid around to sit beside him. His hands slid down to the floor, resting at his sides. The fingers of his left hand found mine, and he toyed with them for a moment, deciding whether he could trust me or not.

"I got an internship at NASA. It's like a program for people like me," he said. "Is that a deal-breaker?"

"A deal-breaker?"

"Yeah." He stared at a glob of gum that was plastered on the carpet, probably decades ago, still toying with my fingers absentmindedly.

"I don't get it. Why would getting an amazing internship be a deal-breaker? And for what, exactly?"

He looked up, a sadness there I didn't expect or care much for. I liked happy Daniel. This Daniel looked like he'd been kicked in the face. "I don't know, never mind. It was a stupid thought. Just don't tell anyone, okay?"

He didn't give me much chance to argue. He stood quickly, pulling me with him. "We need to finish our work if we're ever going to plan this revenge thing."

"Revenge? You mean making Ronin jealous?" I asked.

"Are we still on that? Seriously, Peaches, you deserve better than Ronin McKinsey."

I sighed. "Maybe you're right, but maybe you're wrong. I can't know for sure, not yet anyway. We had a great friendship before we dated. I'm not sure what went wrong, but I need to know, Daniel."

"Why? Why do you want to torture yourself trying to win back someone who doesn't deserve you?" he asked, his personality shifting way too fast for me to keep up anymore.

"Haven't you ever wanted something so much it felt more out of reach than anything? That was Ronin for me. Then suddenly, I had him, then I lost him before I even had a chance to appreciate what we had. That's how I feel, Daniel. I feel like I got all I wanted, then it slipped through my fingers. Maybe he's not the right guy for me in the long run, but I've gotta do this. I have to know for sure."

Daniel licked his lips, a reply there on the tip of his tongue, but instead of saying what was on his mind, he said, "Sure, I guess so."

And that was that. End of conversation. Not another word was uttered about Ronin or prom. It was strictly calculus and French until the store closed. We walked back to the school lot to pick up his bike and my car, all the while, I wondered if I had done something wrong. I was beginning to think he'd changed his mind, not only about the plan but also about our friendship. I couldn't say why; he just... *changed.* The distance between us was uncomfortably vast, and I hated it.

When we reached my car, he nodded and said, "Night, Hazel."

Hazel. No Peaches, just Hazel. I should have let it go, but I couldn't. I got out of the car, slammed the door, and marched up to him as he slid his helmet over his head.

"What is your problem, huh? You talk to me like you're some all-knowing super-human, which makes me feel stupid by the way, then you act like I'm not good enough for you anymore. What's the issue, Daniel? What changed?"

He took his helmet off and tucked it under his arm. "I can't hear a word you're saying with this on. What are you screaming about?"

"Ugh! Darn you, Daniel!" I stomped my foot and turned away from him, but he caught my shoulder and spun me around.

"What? What did I do?"

"You shut me out! You told me your secret, then shut me out. I told you I wouldn't tell anyone, and I'm sorry you regret telling me, but I can't exactly unhear it, now can I?" I felt my lip pucker, and my eyes started to sting, so I bit my lip to hold back the stupid tears.

He put his helmet on the seat of his bike and pulled me into a hug. "I'm sorry. I didn't mean to make you feel that way. I've never told anyone that before besides my family, and it freaked me out," he admitted. "I'm not sure why I even told you, but Peaches, that's not why I shut down."

"Why then?" I mumbled into his shoulder, sniffling.

"I shut down, because I... I like you, Hazel. You're my friend, and I don't want to see you get hurt, especially when it's gonna hurt as much as this will," he said, releasing me from the hug. "But if it's what you truly want, then I'll help you. And Peaches?"

I wiped away the tears that escaped despite my best effort to halt them. "Yeah?" I asked.

"When he screws it up again like I know he will, I'll help you fix the broken bits." He tipped my chin up and forced me to look at him. "I'll always be your friend, no matter what. I trust you, and that means something to me, too."

Seven

Somehow, I knew the moment Daniel said the words that it would happen. I knew Ronin would ruin me before it was all said and done, yet I couldn't stop myself from surging on with the plan. I knew I would break, but maybe that's what I needed. My head knew it was a mistake, but my heart—oh, how my heart wanted to believe Ronin would come back to me. That he would change his mind, and he would suddenly love me again. It would be better than before, and all my worries would be for nothing.

But that's the difference between knowing and caring. I knew, but I didn't care. Perhaps I deserved whatever came my way, but good or bad, I wasn't slowing down. Thank goodness it was Saturday. I could finally take a break from pretending the entire debacle didn't bother me and just be miserable about it.

My father was working a double shift at the hospital, so it was just us girls. Dizzy practically lived at our house, so when she and Rose came into my room in a fit of giggles, I wasn't surprised.

"Hazel, Mom wants to take us shopping. You game?" Rose asked as she poked me in the ribs.

"I don't wanna. I wanna be miserable all day," I whined.

"You didn't seem so miserable with Daniel yesterday," Dizzy said. "What's going on with him?"

"Yes, please, do tell. What's it like to kiss... What is Daniel exactly? A nerd? A bad boy?" Rose asked, working as hard as I had to put Daniel into a neat little box, but I knew better now. Daniel Starnes could not be put into a box because there wasn't a box good enough for him. He was too smart to be categorized, and now that I knew why it made a lot more sense. Nothing about high school was normal for him since he already knew what he was doing for the rest of his life.

"I wouldn't say he's a bad boy or a nerd, more like a... I don't know. Nice," I said.

"He's nice? Is that a category?" Dizzy questioned.

"No, I mean, kissing him is nice. It's... different," I admitted. "It's not like kissing Ronin."

"Is nice a good thing?" Rose asked, and I suddenly realized where their little interrogation was leading.

"Guys, I'm not dating him. We have an arrangement. I get him a date to prom, and he helps me make Ronin jealous. Speaking of prom dates—"

"Do not look at me," Dizzy said. "I hate dances, and I have zero plans to go to prom. Besides, you should go with him."

"Me? No, with any luck, I'll be going with Ronin," I said as I rolled to my side and pushed up. I sat in bed, hair a mess, looking at two people who clearly misjudged the nature of my relationship with Daniel. "Guys, he's helping me with calculus, and I'm helping him with French. Besides that, all we're doing is plotting and scheming."

"Really? How much plotting and scheming has been accomplished?" Dizzy asked.

I thought about it, and come to think of it, we hadn't really come up with a game plan. Besides those few kisses, we'd done nothing, and my plans to set him up with a date for prom blew up in my face left and right.

"Yeah, that's what I thought," she said when I failed to offer a reply. It didn't matter how hard I tried to fight it or to explain why I wanted Ronin back. The two of them were hooked on Daniel, and they weren't letting go any time soon, which was why I was so happy to see my mother appear in my doorway.

"You coming, Hazel? Shopping and lunch, what do you say?" she offered, but I still wasn't feeling it.

"I think I'll pass this time, but thank you," I mumbled, pulling the covers up and settling back into my bed.

"Nope, sorry. It was a rhetorical question, and you answered incorrectly. The whole reason for the trip is to cheer you up, so get your butt up and get dressed so we can go have some fun, child of mine," Mom said, waving her hands as if, magically, it would make me want to move.

I sighed and laid my head on my sister's knee. "You heard the woman. May as well get it over with," Rose said as she played with my hair. "It can't hurt, right?"

"It all hurts, Rose," I said, slowly rising from the comfort of my bed, forced to tackle the day, want to or not. I mumbled and grumbled as I gathered my clothes, then grumbled some more as I showered and dried my hair.

Somehow, we ended up at the mall though I didn't remember much of the ride there. Surprisingly, it didn't take long for me to find my stride with them, rummaging through the racks of clothing, laughing at Dizzy's impression of our history teacher, and listening to my mother crack jokes about my father's snoring habit.

In all, the day hadn't been so bad. It was a slow start, but girl time made it all better. I'd almost forgotten about Ronin McKinsey altogether, but then he had to go and show up—with *her.* It was all very confusing, especially since he'd been swapping spit with another girl the day before, but there was no mistaking that blonde hair. Sara draped herself over him, ignored the uncomfortable look he gave her, and rambled on about who knew what.

"Neither one of them are worth your time, Hazel. You're too good for them," Rose whispered, but the damage was done. Whether I was too good for them or not wasn't the point. I wanted Ronin, and he had clearly moved on.

"She's right. Don't let him do this to you." Dizzy wrapped her arm around my shoulders, turning me away from the sight of my former best friend hanging all over my former boyfriend. All of our other mutual friends were with them. I assumed they were all Ronin's friends now since no one stuck by me. Not one.

"I wonder if Sara wandered into traffic if the rest would follow her?" my mother asked, narrowing her green eyes at Sara. "I might be willing to push her into traffic to test the theory."

"Mom!" Rose exclaimed.

"What? She hurt my daughter. You wait until you have kids, many, many years from now, and you'll see. One day, you'll be tempted to push a teenage girl into traffic for your own child," Mom argued. I loved her for it. There was a small part of me that knew that if I didn't watch her closely, she might seriously consider pushing Sara in front of a semi-truck during rush hour traffic.

"I think it's time for food. Anyone else?" Mom asked.

"Yes, please," I said, dragging my eyes away from the horrific, cliché scene in front of us.

Mom waited until we were elbow-deep in cheeseburgers to begin her speech. She always made sure we had our mouths full before she started those since we would just roll our eyes and argue with her otherwise.

"See, girls, the thing about a broken heart is this... they happen," Mom said with a shrug.

"Brilliant, Mom. Really brilliant," Rose said, rolling her eyes while stealing a few of my waffle fries.

"Hush. Let me finish. All three of you should take notes. Broken hearts happen. It's a fact of life. If you don't get your heart broken at least once in your life, then you haven't truly lived. But you have a choice when it happens. You can let it tear you apart, or you can move on. The world keeps on moving right around your heart, and it doesn't care much how you feel."

"So, shake it off, right?" I asked. Her trademark advice for most of our lives had been to shake it off. If I shook as often as she suggested, I'd shimmy right out of my skin. Get a bad grade? Shake it off. Get into a fight with a friend? Shake it off. Fall from your treehouse when you're eleven and break your arm? Shake it off.

"Heavens no. You don't shake off a broken heart, Hazel. You spackle it back together and try again," she said, placing her fork on the table. "Girls, there's no point in wasting a broken heart. Use it. Learn from it, then put it back together stronger than before, a little wiser, and hopefully give it to the right person the next go-around. The right guy won't care what it looks like or how badly beaten it was before he came along as long as it's his."

"You say that from experience?" Dizzy asked, curiosity eating at her.

"Oh, yes. My heart was blown to smithereens many times before I met the girls' father. It doesn't even hurt to think of those times now because I've found him."

"Easier said than done, I think," I said, stuffing the last fry into my mouth before Rose could steal it.

"I didn't say it was easy, only that it should be done. Now, let's blow this popsicle stand and catch a movie. What do you think?" Mom asked.

Rose and Dizzy were up for it, but I had some thinking to do. I had reached a crossroads, and I wasn't sure which path was the right one for me and my broken, needing to be spackled heart. "I think I need some time alone to think. Can I meet you later?"

"Sure, honey, don't be out too late," Mom said.

"Here," Dizzy said. "Borrow my car. I'm staying over tonight anyway."

I gave her a confused look. "I'm just gonna walk around the mall for a while. I'm not leaving." She shoved the keys at me again.

"Just in case." With that, the three of them went in one direction while I stood trying to decipher the enigma that was Dizzy. I pocketed her keys and began wandering through the mall. I was careful to head in the opposite direction of Ronin and the lemmings. Ronin had seemed downright miserable, yet he didn't push Sara away when she kissed his cheek or draped over him.

And who was the mystery girl in the hall? Why was he kissing her one minute and seemingly with Sara the next? How did he move on so fast? Had he been cheating on me? No, Ronin was a lot of things, but he wasn't a cheater—that much I was sure of.

I knew Ronin was angry when I kissed Daniel, but if he didn't want me, then why was he upset? None of it made any sense, and my head hurt thinking about it. My phone rang, frazzling my nerves. I almost ignored it but thought it could be my mother, so I checked it. It was Daniel. I debated answering the call. Daniel was great, but he wasn't so good at understanding my feelings where Ronin was concerned.

I answered before I could change my mind again. "Hey, Daniel."

"Peaches! I'm bored. Come save me from my boring life," he said dramatically.

"Don't be so dramatic, Dan—" The line went dead before I could respond, and almost immediately, I got a text message from him.

Daniel

> Come over. You can't turn me down through text, Peaches. It's rude.

What a doofus. I certainly could, and it's what I intended to do. I needed time alone to think, and Daniel would be just fine without me. I typed a reply, but just as I was about to tap send, I got another message.

Daniel

> Come over, pleeeeeeaaaase???

I tried to tap send again, but more messages came through.

Daniel

> Please

> Please

> Please

> Please

> Please, with a cherry on top??

I groaned and deleted the message I'd intended to send, then typed another and tapped send before he could barrage me with more begging emojis.

How Dizzy knew I'd leave the mall was beyond me, but it was lucky I had her keys. I barely remembered the way to Daniel's house, probably because I was screaming the last time I rode there, so I had to call him three times to verify I was going the right way. He met me outside, his drama in full force by the time I parked.

"I thought you'd never get here!" He flung himself on me, behaving like a vapored southern belle.

"Where is your sister?" I asked when he finally let me go and led me inside.

"She's with my mom driving to Jacksonville," he said. He was already head-first in the fridge to get me a drink.

"Jacksonville? Florida?"

"Yeah, to the Mayo Clinic. Apparently, there's some experimental treatment for my sister's condition, so they have an interview with them Monday morning," he said, handing me the water and snacks I probably wouldn't eat since the cheeseburger was already settling all wrong.

"Why did she leave so early?" I followed him down the hall to his bedroom, though we had the entire house to ourselves, it seemed.

"I don't know, Peaches. I just live here." Daniel flopped on the bed and flipped on the television. He settled in and patted the space beside him. "I won't bite you. Not too hard, anyway."

I rolled my eyes and sat on the bean bag chair. I took a sip of water, then asked, "What about your Dad? Did he go with them?" It never occurred to me that his family situation was any different from mine—Mom, Dad, sister... maybe a dog—but I was wrong.

"What dad? He bailed when Becca was two years old, and I haven't seen him since," he said as he flipped through the channels. He didn't seem all that shaken over it, but I still felt like a jerk for bringing it up.

"Oh. I didn't know. I'm so sorry."

"Nothing to be sorry about, Peaches. You're not the one who ran off with your much younger assistant, leaving your wife to raise two kids on her own, are you?" He paused the television on a movie we were evidently watching, waiting for my brilliant comeback, but it wasn't coming. I'd never tease him about his father running out.

"Still, I'm sure it's difficult not having a father around." Dig deeper, why don't you, Hazel? I was anxious, so I searched for words to fill the space, but they were all wrong. I didn't want to put him on the spot, but it seemed my brain and my mouth couldn't quite get on the same page.

"Nah, not really. Mom's great, probably better at the dual parenting role than most single moms. She's done a good job playing Dad when necessary, except for that whole debacle with the sex talk. That was awful."

"The... the what?" Surely it wasn't what he meant. I'd heard wrong.

"You know, the birds and the bees? How babies are made and all that?" he asked, waving his hand, indicating that I should be able to keep up with the discussion.

"Your mom gave you the talk? I guess that's not so bad, really." I imagined there were loads of other ways for guys to learn that would be even more uncomfortable than having their mother tell them.

"Yep. Becca and me... at the same time."

And... that would be one of those ways.

"Oh, gosh." I giggled loudly, suppressing the snort I felt coming because I was laughing so hard. "That must have been horrible. I remember when my mom tried to give the talk to Rose and me.

It was a disaster of epic proportions, and when she was done, I swear it felt like she *wanted* us to run out and get pregnant."

Daniel stopped laughing, his stare deathly serious. "Did you?"

I stopped laughing and stared at the insane boy. "Are you serious right now? Have I, at any time, appeared pregnant to you?"

"I don't know. Do you think I spend all my time watching you, Peaches?" His tone sounded disinterested, sarcastic even, but the tint on his cheeks gave me pause. Why was he blushing? This was our usual banter, our *thing* as he called it. I decided I liked the way it looked on his cheeks and wanted to see if I could make it a deeper red.

"I don't know. *Do* you spend all your time thinking about me, Daniel?" I asked, hoping to be rewarded for my efforts with more blushing, but he changed the subject.

He cleared his throat and unpaused the movie. After a few minutes, he said, "Well, at least you didn't screw up and sleep with Ronin." It was an odd statement, one he couldn't have been sure of, and frankly, it was out of line for him to even mention it. When I didn't respond right away, he looked my way with an expression of concern. "Wait... You didn't, did you?"

"Is that really any of your business?" I asked, only slightly offended but far more intrigued by the look of worry on his face. I was glad I hadn't for many reasons, not the least of which was the promise Rose and I had made to each other—we'd wait until marriage, even if it meant breaking up with a guy who wanted something we wouldn't give him.

Daniel realized he'd overstepped and backpedaled. "I suppose not. Sorry. That conversation sort of got away from us, didn't it? Anyway, yeah, Mom plays the role of both parents and Becca—"

"I almost did," I whispered, interrupting him. What was I doing? Why was I about to tell him the truth when thirty seconds ago, I thought it was none of his business?

He sat up straight on the bed, his undivided attention planted on me. "Wh-what?"

"Ronin. I almost did... You know. I planned to the night of our first anniversary, but we both know how that ended, so... I'm glad I didn't, though. I would have broken a promise to my sister if I had... had done that..." I trailed, still unsure why I told him to begin with.

"Oh," he said quietly, his demeanor almost comforting in a quiet, sweet way. He seemed pleased yet afraid to let it show. "Bullet dodged then, I guess."

"Yeah. I guess." I wanted to fall in a hole, any hole would do so long as it was deep and dark.

Daniel reached down and brushed his thumb over my cheek. "Peaches?"

"Yeah?" I whispered.

"It's gonna get better. I promise," he said. "And try not to forget this because it's important—no guy is worth breaking a promise to your sister, and none of us are worth you putting your values on the line for. That said, I *know* the right guy will come along for you." He sat and draped his legs over the edge of his bed while I stayed frozen in the giant bean bag chair.

"How do you know?" I asked.

"Because I know everything," he said with a smirk.

"You don't know everything, Daniel."

"My IQ begs to differ."

I rolled my eyes again. "Just because you're a genius doesn't mean you know everything. What if Ronin never wants to talk to me again?"

"Then it's his loss, and you'll find someone better. Isn't that obvious?"

"You make it sound so easy, but it's not," I argued.

"I make it sound easy because I've done it. It'll hurt for a while, maybe a long while, but eventually, you realize you're not going to get what you want, and you move on. Do yourself a favor, and get through that first phase fast, and the rest will fall into place soon enough." His anger and resentment were evident in the bite of his words. Someone truly hurt him at some point, and despite his argument that he was over it, I suspected he was not.

"Who screwed you over?" I teased. It was meant to be a light and funny question, something to break the tension and force a laugh, but it fell flat. Instead, he explained his position.

"No one really screwed me over. Let's just say I wanted something that someone else got instead, and I spent a lot of time being angry about it. Then one day, I realized I had to move on, or I would always be stuck in this miserable place, watching from afar while some other guy had everything I wanted."

Well, when you finally got Daniel to open up, his high IQ and quirky behavior melded into the background, and a real, human boy emerged.

"I'm sorry, Daniel. I'm sure that was a rough time. For what it's worth, she was crazy if she chose someone else over you."

He raised his head to make eye contact with me. "Yeah?"

"Yes. Absolutely."

"She didn't even notice I existed, so it's not like she chose him over me so much as... I don't know, I guess she overlooked another option," he said.

"How so?" I asked, intrigued. I wasn't sure how much I could get him to spill, but every word was like a deep dive into his mind. I found myself savoring the moment, losing myself in the heartfelt conversation—then he went and broke it.

"Oh, look at the time—"

I lunged forward as if I could somehow catch the lost moment.

"No, Daniel! Not today, you don't. This friendship is a two-way street. If you dig into my life, then you have to give me something in return, and I don't mean telling me you're too smart for your britches!"

"Is that how this works? I've been doing friendship all wrong, too," he said, his grin growing.

"Daniel Starnes," I said with my hand on my hip.

"Okay, okay. She broke my heart, but she never even knew I existed, Peaches. Are you happy now? I tried to get her attention. I really did, like a thousand times, but she never saw me. She fell for some other guy, and if she'd ripped my heart out and danced on it, it wouldn't have hurt as much as watching her walk into the sunset with him. Do you know why?"

I shook my head, unable to form an actual word. He was still hurt by it, whether he chose to admit it or not, and it sort of made me want to find this girl and rip her throat out.

"Because he never deserved her, and now I'm watching my best friend make the same stupid mistake of pining after someone who isn't coming back. Ronin walked away, Peaches. Accept it and move on."

All I heard was what he called me—his best friend.

"Your best friend?" I asked.

"Yeah, that's you, Peaches. You're the idiot best friend who's gonna get hurt."

"I'm your best friend?" I asked, pointing to myself.

"Well, I don't have any other friends, so don't feel too special." He grabbed me by the wrist and helped me the rest of the way up from the floor. "Let's go."

"Where are we going?" I asked as he slipped his shoes on.

"Fire and Ice."

"No, I don't want to go there, Daniel. I can't." No way, and no how was I going there. Ronin was probably there with Sara right that second.

"Do you like the place? Do you like eating cake and ice cream, Peaches?" Daniel met me in the middle of the room, his eyebrows arched as he waited for my reply.

I sighed. "I do, but—"

"Well, Ronin doesn't get to keep it in the divorce, not if you don't let him have it. I'm going. Are you going with me?" He walked to his door, waiting for me in the doorway. It was the crossroads again. A choice to be made. I could wallow in misery, or I could start spackling. Ice cream was an excellent way to start spackling.

I took his outstretched hand. "I'm in. Feed me all the ice creams, Daniel."

Eight

As far as bad ideas went, Daniel's idea to go to Fire and Ice was probably the worst, but I was already two scoops into my chocolate ice cream when Ronin walked in. There was no going back. It was the last stand, as Daniel had said seven times on the way there. Ronin was with a group, Sara and Tee included, and he saw me the second he walked in the door. Sara was too busy stinking up the place with her strawberry-scented body lotion to notice me, but Ronin did.

Daniel wanted to sit in the corner booth, the one I always shared with Ronin, to really stick it to him where it would hurt, but I didn't want to. One might think it was because I didn't want to tarnish the memories I had made with Ronin in that corner booth, but in truth, it felt more like tarnishing the friendship I was building with Daniel. Tee saw me sitting along the wall, chocolate ice cream melting on my spoon as I debated taking a bite or running into the bathroom like a baby.

He broke from the group and came to our table. "Hey, Hazel, how's it goin'?"

"Uh... good?" I ate the ice cream, so I would have a moment to come up with something more intelligent to say.

"Daniel, right?" Tee asked Daniel, then pointed to a chair asking permission to sit.

"Yeah, the one and only. Well, there are those other two Daniels, but they're freshmen." Daniel shrugged, and Tee laughed. He pulled out the chair and sat when no one told him not to, and I caught Ronin staring at us again. Or maybe he was trying to figure out why his best friend was sitting with his ex-girlfriend and her... whatever he thought Daniel was.

"Cool, so I've been wondering how you're doing. The last time we talked...," he trailed off when Daniel wrapped his arm around me and pulled me closer.

"I'm fine, Tee, really. I was sort of a mess before, but things are okay." The ease with which I delivered the lie was astounding, even to me. "Daniel's been great."

Tee glanced at Daniel, a little concern on his face, but it was fleeting. Daniel smiled at him as he rubbed my arm. "That's good. I'm glad to hear that. Listen, I've gotta get back to the guys, but maybe we can catch up sometime?" Tee asked.

"Sure, I guess so." I couldn't figure out why Ronin's best friend would want to catch up with his ex, but maybe Tee had been truthful when he said I was his friend too.

"Maybe we could catch a movie or something? You know, like, maybe a double date or something?" he asked, pushing in his chair with awkward slowness, stalling. As far as I knew, Tee was single. I was sure he wasn't asking me out, not with Daniel essentially staking a flag on my head and calling me his.

"Okay..." I said, confused.

Tee sighed, and his shoulders slouched. "Okay, I'm trying to ask you if it's okay to ask your sister out. I really like her, but I didn't want to make things weird for you." He tapped his fingers on the back of the chair, all the while Ronin watched from afar. Sara was annoyed. She kept trying to get Ronin's attention, but his gaze was settled on the three of us.

"Oh," I said, taken by surprise. "I think that's okay. I mean, it's not like you're bringing Ronin along," I said. Daniel snickered beside me, reminding me I should probably make sure he was okay with pretending to be my boyfriend in front of my sister and Tee.

"Would that be okay with you, Daniel?" I asked with as breezy a tone as possible. *Just another day making plans with friends, Hazel. You can do this.*

"Sure, babe. Whatever you want." Daniel continued to eat his cake with very little interest in what Tee and I discussed but kept his arm protectively around me.

"Are you sure? Because you're my friend, and I don't want things to be any more difficult for you than they already are," Tee insisted.

"She's good. She's got me. Ronin's old news. We're free tonight if you want," Daniel said, wiping chocolate frosting from his face.

Tee waited for my reaction before speaking. "Sure, it's good. If you want, I can ask Rose to join us and set you up. Unless, of course, you'd like to ask her out yourself?"

"Uh... No, it's fine. I'll just give her a call. Thanks, Hazel, for being so cool about this," Tee said, but he was watching Daniel the whole time.

"Any time. I'm sure Rose will be excited about it," I said. I had no idea whether she would or not, but I didn't know what else to say. At that point, all I could do was hope she liked him enough to go on a date with him and that she would keep her mouth shut about the deal I had with Daniel.

Tee nodded, then went to join his group again, and all the while, Ronin watched. He whispered to Tee, who turned around and looked back at us, then shook his head yes and sat down beside Tanner.

"Wait for it," Daniel said. "I'll bet you another bowl of ice cream."

"What?" I asked. "What are we betting on?"

"I'm going to the bathroom, and I guarantee he's over here before the door shuts behind me."

"Wait, no, don't leave me here!" It was too late. Daniel was already out of the booth and headed toward the bathroom. Just as he predicted, Ronin slid from Sara's grip and moseyed over to my table as casually as possible. He pretended to be scouring the cases for a tasty treat, but he should have known me better than that. I knew him. He always ordered the same thing—always.

"Hi, Hazel," Ronin said, casually and halfway watching the bathroom door. I lifted my head from my ice cream, which was more of a soup than anything at that point.

"Oh, hi, Ronin." I busied myself with wiping up dribbles from the table and the hundreds of crumbs Daniel dropped while eating his cake.

"You look nice," Ronin said, shuffling his feet. Small talk, excellent.

"Thanks, you too." I crossed my arms in front of me, a defensive maneuver I was sure he picked up, but I had to either cross my arms or strangle him. Only one didn't land me in jail.

"Um, listen, I wanted to tell you... I... I really miss you, and I'm sorry for—"

"Ronin! What are you doing?" Sara yelled across the shop. "Are you getting my ice cream?"

"In a minute!" Ronin yelled back with a frustrated groan. He gave his attention back to me and said, "I wanted to apologize for the way we broke up. It was—"

"Humiliating? Embarrassing? Mortifying? I could go on if you like." I found a little backbone, where I didn't know—maybe the same place I found my pride—but once I found it, I decided to use some of it.

"I know, really, it was awful. I was so sticky—"

"I meant for me, Ronin, not for you." I tossed the napkin on the table and stood to face him. "If you wanted to break up, fine, but the way you did it was uncalled for, and I have nothing else to say to you." What was I doing? There he was, pouring his heart out, and I stomped it to bits! The moment I was waiting for was right there in front of me!

"That's what I meant, Hazel. It was awful the way I treated you, and I'm genuinely sorry. I miss you, and I was hoping we could talk. I'd like to be able to be in the same place as you and not feel this giant elephant sitting on my chest." He didn't say he wanted to get back together, but he also didn't say he *didn't* want to. I was so confused.

"Talk about what?" I asked.

"Us, how this is going to work. We have mutual friends, Hazel, and—"

"We have one mutual friend, and he seems fine with juggling us the way we are now," I said. Tee watched the conversation unfold, but the rest didn't have a care in the world. Ronin could keep the others. I'd make new, better friends—save Tee, who was possibly the sweetest person on the planet.

"Okay, then, just us. We were friends once, and I'm not sure what happened," Ronin said.

His voice wore me down, gentle and apologetic, and I found myself agreeing to talk. "Fine, call me tomorrow after lunch."

He smiled, the one I knew meant he was delighted. "Really? Okay, great. Tomorrow after lunch."

"Ronin!"

"I'm coming!" he yelled back at my former friend, whose panties were all in a tizzy. It was impossible to wipe the satisfied smirk off my face, and I had a good feeling it was equally impossible for Sara to hide her anger.

Ronin started to back away just as Daniel came back from the restroom. Daniel slid into the booth beside me with his goofy smile. "Ready to go?"

"Yeah, I was just talking to Ronin, but I'm ready."

Daniel sat beside me, questioningly, waiting patiently for me to give him a clue as to what he should be doing while we both sat in front of Ronin. Well, that was easy to answer. He should be kissing me, of course.

I leaned forward a fraction of an inch, and Daniel closed the gap. It was short and sweet, but it sent a message. I was with someone else. I was no longer with Ronin McKinsey. The thing was, I was so focused on that small, sweet kiss that I never noticed Ronin storm out of Fire and Ice like his pants were literally on fire. Not until Daniel said something.

"That hit him in the ouchy spot, I think. Nice job, Peaches."

"Huh?" I glanced around, still lost in the euphoria of the kiss, and noticed Ronin was missing. "Oh... Mission accomplished, I guess."

"Are you okay?" Daniel narrowed his eyes and leaned his head down a bit to get a better view of my face.

Was I okay? I wasn't sure, and being unsure made me feel weaker than ever. I felt tears stinging my face, but I didn't understand why. Ronin said he missed me, he wanted to talk to me—those should have been good things that made me happy, yet I felt worse than I had the day he broke up with me. My emotions were all over the place, and I couldn't see which end was up.

"Peaches?" Daniel brushed his fingers over mine, bringing me back to reality. I brushed it off as quickly as I could.

"Yeah, yeah, I'm all good. Why don't we go back to my house and annoy my sister?" I offered.

"Sure, I have a lot of annoying to do since my sister is out of town, so I guess I could use it up on your sister," he said, shrugging as if it was all the same to him. Any sister would do.

And that's precisely what he did. He meddled with Rose's things, making comments about the science project that still grew on the plate, poking her in the ribs when she least expected it, trying to read her journal—all manner of things I imagined a big brother would do to annoy the snot out of his sister on purpose. Eventually, Rose threw us out of her room.

We settled in my room for a while, but when I left for five seconds and returned, Daniel was gone. I found him sitting on our kitchen island, hands flailing around and mouth moving a mile a minute. My mother would periodically stuff a cookie in his mouth so she could speak, but the second he was finished chewing, he was at it again.

"So, I said, 'Hazel, it's just a bear,' but she insists there's a tiny old man stuck inside." I heard him say and decided it was time to intervene before my mother put me in an institution.

"I think you have that story backward," I said, snatching my mother's homemade chocolate chip cookie from his hand.

"Hey! I was gonna eat that," he said with a pout. My mother handed him more cookies with a sly smile, one that said she knew there was something more than friendship going on, but she couldn't have been more off-base.

"I like this one. Let's keep him," Mom said, then turned her attention back to her cookie baking.

"He's not a stray dog, Mom." I hopped up on the island beside Daniel, and she immediately went bonkers.

"Off the counter!" she yelled, whacking at me with her spatula.

"He's on the counter!" I said.

"I like him," she said, patting his knee. "You drive me nuts six and a half days a week. Start listening to me when I tell you about my day, and I might let you sit on the counter."

Daniel smiled, cookie crumbs falling from his face. The little brat. I was suddenly grateful I didn't have a brother. It was clear my mother wasn't letting him leave the kitchen any time soon. It was also painfully clear that I was not smart enough to understand their conversation about why Pluto should or should not be a planet, so I found my way back to my sister's bedroom.

"Daniel leave?" Rose asked with a somewhat hopeful tone to her voice.

"No, I think Mom's gonna adopt him," I said, flopping on the bed beside Dizzy. She was staring up at the ceiling at something, and the second I looked, it splatted on my face. "Ahh!" I yelled.

"Calm down, it's just a splat ball," Dizzy said, peeling the slimy ball off my face. She tossed it up to the ceiling again, it splatted and stuck, then slowly peeled away a little at a time. "So, lover boy is impressing Mama Simmons. That's good."

I rolled my eyes. "He's not my boyfriend. Seriously, get off that. Oh, hey Rose, did Tee call you today?" I sat up in the bed in time to see Rose stiffen. Her head slowly turned toward me.

"Why? Did he say he was calling? Did you talk to him? Did he ask about me? What did he—"

"Whoa, are you telling me you like him, and you haven't told me?" I asked, a little hurt but mostly excited. A guilty look passed over her face, and Dizzy sat up beside me.

"She wasn't sure how you'd take it, him being idiot's best friend and all," Dizzy said, a question in her voice. She was also worried, but I was genuinely happy for my sister. Tee was a great guy, and Rose deserved a great guy.

"Ooh, are we having girl talk?" Daniel threw himself on the bed so hard I slid off the edge, but Dizzy managed to hold on. She shot him a warning look. If he started the whole brother bit again, he was out. Not just out, but out-out. She'd toss him on the street in a nanosecond.

"Yes, and you're not a girl, so—" Rose started.

"But I was there when Tee asked Hazel if he could ask you out, so technically—"

"Daniel!" I shouted. "Way to ruin it for her!"

Rose jumped Daniel like a lion on a steak. "What did he say about me? Do you think he really likes me? You're a guy, you would know, right? Tell me!" Dizzy peeled Rose from Daniel, whose eyes were the size of saucers.

Once Rose was a safe distance from him, Daniel slid into the corner. "I don't like this girl talk thing," he mumbled.

"That's why you don't interrupt a group of besties when they're talking about boys," Dizzy said.

"But I'm Hazel's best friend, so how does that work?" Daniel argued.

"I'm her sister. I'm first," Rose informed him. "Everyone else falls in line behind me."

"Yeah, and I'm Rose's best friend, which makes me Hazel's by default." Dizzy gave Daniel a breakdown of how she saw the hierarchy of best friendship. It was all news to me as well, but the look on Daniel's face was funny enough to let it continue without questioning Dizzy's crazy ways.

"No, no, no. Okay, I concede that Rose is number one. She's the sister, but there is no way you're number two. Ha-ha, number two," Daniel got side-tracked for a moment but came back strong. "She spends all her time with me now, so I'm her best non-sibling friend."

"But I know more about her; therefore, I am the second-best." Dizzy knew full well she was irritating him, but it was his payback for annoying her.

"No, no chance. Peaches is my best friend. She's the only friend I have, which, mathematically and theoretically, makes it impossible for her to be anyone else's best friend but mine."

"Your argument makes no sense whatsoever. It's a load of number two. I've known her since elementary school, and you've known her what, like, three days?" Dizzy scoffed while Rose and I sat back and watched the show.

"Psshht... Try, like, four days, but if you take that four days and multiply it by the number of heartfelt conversations we've had, add the number of times we ticked off her ex together, square that by the root of how many times we've kissed, times the number of balloons she'll blow up for my birthday, carry the seven, and you get... dun, dun, dun... one. Which is me. I'm number one!"

"Your math is flawed."

"My math is perfect, isn't it Peaches?"

Both looked to me to settle the argument. I was put on the spot, not having a clue what to say about two people arguing over me. Lately, people have been working overtime to ditch me from their lives as quickly as possible, so the turn of events was flattering yet confusing.

"Um..."

"I'm kidding. Peaches can have as many best friends as she wants. She's too awesome to keep to myself," Daniel said, causing Dizzy to whip her head around so fast she nearly fell from the bed a second time. When she was finished assessing

Daniel's sincerity, she looked back at me. Her expression was clear—don't screw it up.

"I like him much better than Ronin. Don't screw it up," she said. I forgot Dizzy always said what she was thinking, which was why her comment caught me off-guard.

"We're just friends, right Peaches?" Daniel smiled and started flipping through one of Rose's magazines. I didn't like the statement. It hit me all wrong, the idea of being *just* friends. Surely, there was more to our friendship than the word *just* implied, but what was it? Somehow, he felt like more than a friend but less than... My thought was interrupted by Rose's phone ringing.

"Oh, gosh. It's him. What do I do?" Rose asked me.

"Answer it," Daniel said, annoying Rose again.

"I mean, what should I say?" she asked.

"Say hello." Daniel had no idea how close he was to the end of his life, but Dizzy did, and she distracted him with more magazines.

"I guess what he said. He really is going to ask you out. He asked me if it was okay, and I said yes. He wants us to double date, so answer the phone already!" I said, pushing it closer to her.

She answered and immediately slipped into a zombie-like state. She mumbled; she stuttered; she stammered, and, eventually, she said yes. "I'm such an idiot," she said when she hung up the phone.

"Sometimes guys like idiots," Daniel said, and that was it for Rose. She yelled and sprang from the floor, pouncing on him and jabbing her thin fingers into his ribs. He tried to fight her off, but he failed, and she tickled him until he was purple. When she finally let him up for air, I couldn't stop laughing.

"Is it funny?" Daniel asked. "Do you think it's still funny now?" He leaped at me, pinning me to the ground and tickling me until I couldn't breathe, but Dizzy, the friend that she was, tackled him to the ground. Before long, my mother had to intervene—probably because she had a serious issue with us duct-taping Daniel to the chair to tickle him.

"Crap, we have half an hour to get ready!" Rose yelped and darted to the bathroom.

"I'll help," Dizzy said and ran off to catch Rose.

"Oh, boy! Is this the part where I get to learn about make-up and shoes?" Daniel teased, so I plastered the duct tape over his mouth. He mumbled something incoherent, so I ripped the tape back off to hear better.

"Ahhh! Why did you do that?" he yelled. "I was giving you a compliment!"

"Oops, sorry, couldn't hear you," I said flippantly. Daniel was still sitting in the chair with no one else around, no one to impress, just the two of us. He had no one to make jealous, no one to make a show for, no reason to give me a compliment. He just... *wanted* to.

"I was trying to be nice and look what you did," he said, pointing to the red mark on his face.

"Okay, what was it then?" I asked, a bit nervous though I had no clue why.

"Wear that red dress, the one with the little sparkly belt thing," he said. "You look really beautiful in that."

"The dress I wore to Josh Salazar's party last summer?" I purchased the dress for that party, and I hadn't worn it since. I barely remembered it myself, and I didn't remember seeing Daniel at that party—not that I would. I'd only realized he existed after the fire alarm incident.

"Yeah, that one." The tint on his cheeks returned. I thought there was probably no harm in wearing it. Besides, the dress would probably drive Ronin crazy, too. Red was his favorite color, after all.

"That's a good idea. It'll drive Ronin nuts," I said.

"I think it'll drive any guy in a five-mile radius nuts, Peaches," he said, then left the room so I could get ready.

I found the dress in the back of my closet, a little wrinkled, but it would fall out with some wear. I slipped it on and buckled the glittery belt, appreciating the suggestion. I left my hair down, but ran a blow dryer over it to liven it up, then painted my lips red. A little mascara—okay, maybe three coats for good measure—and voila!

It felt good to doll up a little, even if it wasn't a real date. Ronin never really liked it when I wore heels. He said it made him feel short, but Daniel was easily eight inches taller than me, so I slipped them on without worry. I was probably overdressed for a movie, but when I walked into the hall and saw Rose just as dressed up, I felt better about it.

Dizzy whispered in my ear, "Someone is staring at you."

I glanced down the hall where Daniel was waiting. My mother had loaned him one of my father's shirts so we wouldn't have to go by his house on the way. He looked great. A simple button-down shirt paired with his usual jeans. He'd even run a comb through his hair, an attempt to control the messiness that failed but still looked so amazing on him.

"Um..." I stuttered, realizing I was staring at him, too. "Should we go? We don't want to be late."

"You look... I mean... Do we *have* to go out tonight?" Daniel asked, ignoring the fact that my sister and Dizzy were standing right there.

"Why? Are you feeling okay? Is something wrong?" I asked.

He shook his head a little, then offered me his hand. "Nothing. No, I'm fine. Let's go have some fun." I took his hand, nothing we hadn't done a million times before, and he led me to the front door with Rose trailing behind us. Dizzy was totally fine hanging out with our mother until we returned, one of the reasons she was such a great friend.

The other reason? Her ability to make me see something I hadn't before. She pulled me aside and motioned for Daniel to go ahead. "Daniel, she'll be right out. I just remembered I need to ask her something."

"Cool, shall we?" Daniel offered Rose his arm, which she took with a sarcastic little smirk. The two left through the front door, leaving me alone with Dizzy.

"Hazel, please don't screw this up. Whatever it is you think you have to do with Ronin, let it go. Just let it go," she urged.

"Dizzy, I appreciate—"

"Did you not see that? Are you as blind as you are stupid when it comes to boys?"

"Excuse me?" I asked indignantly. How dare she call me... Okay, I was stupid when it came to boys.

"Oh, don't play games with me. You know I'm right. Just do me a favor, one favor, and I'll stop annoying you about Daniel and Ronin."

I sighed. "Fine, what is it?"

"When you walk out that door, forget about Ronin. For one night, forget about him entirely. No deal with Daniel, no making Ronin jealous, no getting him back. Forget it all for just one night—tonight." With that, she shoved me out the door.

She was an odd duck, too, that Dizzy. But she was also smart. I did just as she asked, only because I wanted to make a point. I wanted to prove that Ronin was right for me, and her ridiculous thoughts of Daniel swooping in to steal my heart away were just that—ridiculous.

I got into the passenger seat of my own car, letting Daniel drive us to the theater to meet Tee. Rose and Daniel were already in the middle of a conversation about the movie we were headed to see—already more than she and Ronin ever spoke, so when I settled in, I didn't interrupt them. His eyes lit up, a brilliant green I couldn't stop staring at. Hazel eyes... Daniel laughed at what my sister said—not fake, a real laugh. He glanced at me and gave me an appreciative smile, really seeing me. At least, it felt that way since no one had ever looked at me that way before.

"You look beautiful, Peaches," he said, then gave his attention back to Rose.

Crooked smile, pretty eyes. Daniel made me laugh a lot, smile more than most, and didn't give a care about what anyone thought about him. Solid, that's what I saw when I looked at Daniel. Someone reliable, someone I could trust and count on when I needed him.

I didn't know how Dizzy knew. I couldn't say how she figured it all out. But just as sure as I sat there, I was falling for Daniel Starnes.

"You okay, Peaches?" he asked, glancing at me once more before he put the car in drive.

I nodded and clicked my seatbelt into place. *Click.* Just a little click, the sound of a big, fat realization falling on my head. I liked Daniel. I liked Daniel a lot, and Ronin McKinsey was slowly fading into the background.

Nine

- -

To say I didn't care at all about Ronin was an overstatement. It wasn't entirely true. That, coupled with my insecurities, made me talk myself out of Daniel as an option before we'd even set foot in the movie theater. The fact was, Daniel was a genius, and I was not—not even close. Daniel had his future mapped out. He knew what he wanted, and I was not part of that plan. He said as much himself when he said we were *just friends*.

Geez, Hazel. Why do you do these things to yourself? I loved an idiot, and I was falling for a genius. Neither wanted me as anything more than an ex-girlfriend or a friend, respectively. Whatever Dizzy saw, or thought she saw, was probably far more one-sided than she realized.

I caught Daniel staring at me, which was naughty since he was supposed to be driving. "Peaches, seriously, are you okay?"

"Yeah, I'm fine. A little tired, that's all," I said, not a total lie. I was tired—tired of trying to figure boys out, of guessing what it was about me that made them run away screaming, of trying to change who I was to make everyone else happy while I slowly realized I was miserable.

Daniel pulled into the lot and parked. I saw Tee waiting by the ticket booth on the phone, but he hung up when he saw us approaching.

"Wow, you guys look great," he said, causing Rose to live up to her name with a pinkish tinge to her cheeks.

"Thanks," Daniel said.

Tee tore his eyes from my sister and looked at Daniel. "I meant the... Oh, never mind. I went ahead and got four tickets since the line was getting long." He handed Daniel two tickets and started talking to Rose, leaving me to come up with something to say to Daniel. It wasn't a date, but it was to everyone else watching. It was a non-date date that I wished was a date but wasn't. See? Tired.

"I wish you'd tell me what's bothering you. Maybe I can help?" Daniel asked, slipping his fingers through mine. It wasn't necessary to show so much affection since Ronin was nowhere to be found, but he did it anyway. Maybe it's what he imagined best friends did. Curse Dizzy and her mouth. Now I questioned every move Daniel made, wondering if it was part of the plan, just something we did as friends, or something else entirely.

"I really am tired," I said, faking a yawn that turned into a real one.

"You can nap on my shoulder if you want, or I can take you home. I don't think they'll miss us much." He pointed over his shoulder at Rose and Tee, who were lost in conversation. I really didn't want to bail on my sister, but the thought of sitting with Daniel next to me for two hours, debating his feelings in my head, made me want to vomit.

My loyalty to my sister overruled my insecurity. It would prove to be a difficult movie to watch, though. Too much gore and guts for my taste, which meant I regularly covered my eyes or shoved my face into Daniel's shoulder, waiting for the blood to disappear from the screen. He didn't seem to mind, but every time I did it, I felt silly. It was all very ridiculous to fall for a guy I'd only known a few days. He was just being kind and helping me out, and in return, he would get a prom date out of the deal. That was it. He was kind, and I needed a nice, sweet friend—not a boyfriend whose brain I would never understand.

"Excuse me, I need to use the ladies' room," I said, unsure if I was excusing myself because the movie made me want to puke or because I wanted to clear my mind of Daniel.

"Do you need me to come with you?" Daniel asked.

"I've been going potty unassisted for many years, so I think I'm good," I said, mortifying myself as the words fell from my mouth. What an idiot. My brain was not even in the same realm as his, let alone the same room.

He smirked. "Well, I could—"

"Do not finish that sentence. Whatever it was, do not finish it," I said.

"I was gonna say I could go get some more snacks while you're gone, but now I'm curious to know what gutter your mind is in?" he asked, irritating the man behind him, who shushed him, only making Daniel speak louder. "Maybe another bucket of popcorn would be nice!"

"Shh, Daniel!" I fussed as I walked away as fast as I could. My face probably looked like a giant tomato. I didn't have to go, but I did need to regain my composure. Thinking of Daniel as anything other than a friend, a best friend, was moronic on so many levels. Back to plan A, get him a date, and get Ronin back.

Ronin and I were better suited to one another, and I had a feeling when I saw him again, all those old feelings would return in full force. I managed to pry myself away from Daniel long enough to slip into the empty ladies' room, give myself a pep talk, and fix my makeup. Once my mind was somewhat clear, I reminded myself one last time that Daniel did not need his best friend to fall for him and headed toward the door.

I opened the bathroom door, and of course—because my life was one cliché drama after another—there was Ronin. He stood at the snack counter, tapping his debit card on the glass countertop. Tanner and Sara were with him, but Sara didn't look very thrilled about it.

Sara glanced my way just as I was retreating into the safety of the bathroom again. I'd just lock myself in there for two or three hours, long enough for them to see their movie and leave. If I was lucky, Sara didn't recognize me, and I would be just fine. I forgot I was a hugely unlucky person.

Sara threw the door open, almost smacking me in the face with it. "Oh, I didn't see you there."

She walked to the mirror to freshen up, and I noticed a few new things about her. Her blonde hair was a lot blonder, her eyelashes a lot faker, her lip gloss a bright shade of pink, and her clothes were a size too small. Perhaps it was an attempt to keep Ronin's eyes on her alone, but if a clown car had rolled through the bathroom to pick her up, it wouldn't have surprised me. She looked ridiculous. If she knew Ronin at all, she'd have known that was not what he liked.

"What are you staring at?" she snapped.

"Nothing. Nothing at all," I said, pulling the door open to escape the strawberry-lotion-scented ex-friend of mine.

She pushed the door closed, and with one long pointy finger, she poked my chest. "Listen, Hazel, and listen close. Ronin is mine now. You had your chance, and you screwed it up, so stay away from my boyfriend."

"Funny, your boyfriend wants to talk to me about getting back together tomorrow at lunch. Did you know that?" I wasn't sure that's what Ronin wanted to discuss, but I didn't care. It made her mad, and that was the point.

She laughed. "No, he wants to meet you to apologize for being mean, which he wasn't. You were a freak, but for some reason, he feels bad about how things happened."

"Whatever, Sara. Are you done now? I'm here with friends."

"What friends, Hazel?" she asked in a sing-song voice that made me want to flush her head down a toilet. A stall door opened, and a girl our age stepped out. I hadn't even noticed she was there until she appeared at the sink station, which meant she had heard my personal pep talk and, well, all the other crazy things I said to myself before Sara. Poor girl, she'd probably stayed in the safety of the stall as long as she could in the presence of crazy people.

Sara rolled her eyes at her, irritated she interrupted our little spat. "Just stay away from him. Am I clear?"

With that, she stomped out the door in a whirl of strawberry stink. The girl, dressed in a theater uniform, washed her hands in silence. Once she was finished, she pulled a few towels from the dispenser and gave me a look.

"I um... tried to stay in there as long as I could to mind my own business, but that whole thing was awkward. It seemed like you needed an escape." She shrugged and smiled. She'd saved my life and my sanity just by walking out of a bathroom stall. "Anyway, she was super-pleasant. What did you do to get on her good side?"

I chuckled sarcastically. "I got dumped."

"Ahh, say no more. I know the type. Let me guess. She's your former best friend turned boyfriend stealing arch-nemesis?" She tossed the towels in the trash and leaned against the wall, killing time.

"You forgot, she also stole my position as cheer captain," I said, leaning against a stall door to seem as casual and laid-back as she did. Bad idea. It flew in, and I tripped, falling onto the floor with a thud. My butt hurt, but my head hurt even more. One should never, ever hit her head on a toilet seat.

"Oh, gosh! Are you okay?" She helped me up and looked me over. "I can get you some ice for that bump, then we'll fill out an accident report."

"Oh, no, no report. I'm clumsy. It was all my fault."

"Still, I'll get you the ice. That's gonna hurt for a while." She escorted me out, and I waited by the employee door while she got the ice. She handed it to me, wrapped in a towel. "Here, I also snagged these for you. Maybe you can use them on a night super-pleasant ex-bestie isn't here."

She handed me two movie tickets with a smile. "My name's Natalie, by the way."

"I'm Hazel, and thanks for this. It was really nice of you," I said just as I heard Sara whining about something the poor guy behind the counter did wrong. Bless his soul, he deserved a medal for dealing with her.

"Does she have an off button, seriously? She reminds me of *my* ex-best friend, always telling me what to do and whining when she didn't get her way."

"You know what, now that you mention it, she has always been on the whiny side." I contemplated my friendship with Sara and realized it had all been very one-sided, and she often made a big deal out of the smallest things.

The guy behind the counter apologized profusely as Ronin tried to convince him it was not his fault.

"I'm the shift manager," Natalie said. "I should go see what's going on. Go enjoy your movie, Hazel."

I thanked her again and turned on my heel to go. I heard Natalie speaking to Sara, apologizing for the miscommunication and informing her that they would fix her order immediately. Just as I was about to turn the corner to head back to the theater, I heard Sara squeal. A quick glance, and I saw Natalie holding back a smirk as she said, "Oh, no! I'm so, so sorry! I guess the lid wasn't on tight enough!"

Sara stood in a puddle of red slush, her blonde hair stained red and her perfect outfit covered with the icy drink. I laughed, catching Sara's attention as well as Ronin's and Natalie's. Natalie gave me a thumbs up, the devious little thing, and Sara stormed out the front door, trailing slush behind her.

Ronin's eyes settled on me, and he smiled—a small smile, but it was still for me. Tanner couldn't stop laughing at Sara as he tugged on Ronin's shirt sleeve, distracting him from me. I'd been gone a while, and Rose must have grown concerned. She appeared at my side in time to see Tanner and Ronin leaving.

"You okay?" she asked.

"Never better, Rose. Never better," I said.

Sara was a slushy-covered mess. Ronin wanted me back clear as day, and I might have found a new friend in Natalie. At the very least, I owed her a huge thank you. She single-handedly improved my mood with one dumped slushy.

"What happened?" Daniel asked, standing behind Rose. "You disappeared. I thought you left us."

"No, why would I do that?" I asked. Daniel watched closely; the change in my mood was evident even to him. "I wouldn't leave my best friend behind, Daniel."

Even as I said it, it didn't feel quite right. But it made him smile, which only solidified my position. He wanted a friend, not a girlfriend in Hazel Simmons. He took my hand, something

I decided was a gesture of friendship, and led me back to the theater. Thank goodness, the movie was almost over.

Just before the ending credits, Daniel leaned over and whispered, "Why don't we give them some alone time and take a walk, maybe go to our place?" I nodded my approval and slid out of the seat. Natalie was busy with customers, so I decided I'd thank her the next time we came in. Thinking of what she did made me smile.

"What's so funny?" Daniel asked.

"That lovely girl over there," I said, pointing to Natalie. "Her name is Natalie, and I think I love her to death."

"Well, this all took a sudden turn," he said.

I smacked his arm. "She dumped a slushy on Sara's head. That's what I was watching while you were watching people get dismembered," I said.

"Aw, I missed that? I think I love her, too," he said.

A thought popped into my head. "Hey, maybe you can ask her to prom? She seems nice. I mean, after the whole argument with Sara in the bathroom and whacking my head on the toilet, she was really sweet and helpful."

Daniel stopped at the door, his hand hovering over the handle. "Wait... What the heck happened in the bathroom?"

"Oh, I didn't get to tell you everything. I saw Ronin, Tanner, and Sara in the lobby when I came out of the bathroom. Sara saw me, so I tried to get away, but she cornered me in the bathroom with her silly threats—"

"She *threatened* you?" Daniels' eyes flamed a deep golden color. I'd never seen eyes that color *at all,* so I kept staring at them until he turned away. He pushed open the door and took my hand with a grumble. We started walking toward our place as I continued my story.

"No, she didn't *threaten* my life or anything. She was just saying stupid stuff, nothing to worry about." I waved it off and continued with the part about Natalie. "So, this girl, Natalie, she was in the stall and heard the whole thing go down. When she came out, Sara left in a huff. Long story short, Natalie made a few comments about how annoying Sara's behavior was, and I slipped, fell, and cracked my noggin on the toilet."

Daniel stopped short. "I thought you said you didn't need help in the bathroom?"

"I don't."

"One who slips and cracks their skull on a toilet most certainly needs supervision when peeing," he said but found it challenging to keep a straight face while he did so.

"Anyway, we got to talking, and she gave me these." I handed him the tickets Natalie had given me. "So, she got annoyed with Sara because she was mean to another employee, and she dumped a slushy on her head, which was hilarious. You should have seen it. And I was thinking, maybe we can come back next week, and I can thank her properly for making my day. Then, you can ask her to prom?"

"You want me to ask a total stranger I have never spoken a word to, to prom?" he asked.

"Sure, why not? She seems great, plus bonus points for ruining Sara's night," I argued.

"I'm not asking a total stranger to prom, Peaches."

"You kissed a total stranger, Daniel. What's the difference?"

"When did I... Oh, that's way different. When I kissed you, at least I knew you went to our school and you weren't weird. I mean, I'm still not sure about that last part, but going to prom with a stranger is different," he said, suddenly picking up the pace. The bookstore would close in an hour, and I guessed he wanted a snack.

"How is it different?" I asked, curious.

"I kissed you, that's way different than asking someone to go to a dance and stare at me for four hours."

"Stare at you? What, exactly, do you think happens at prom?" I was beginning to think his social ineptness was far greater than I'd realized.

"You know what I mean. Dancing, talking, blah, blah, blah," he said. "None of that is fun with a total stranger."

"You sound like you don't really want to go. What's the deal?" I asked. We stepped into the store, and I followed him to the back corner—the one where he told me his secret. Was that our thing, too? Did we tell each other our secrets in dark corners of little, dusty bookstores with old man bears watching us?

He sat on the floor and reclined against the shelf. I tried to sit, but... short dress.

"Here, come here." He offered his hand. When I took it, he pulled me onto his lap. With his legs crossed, there was enough elevation that I could sit comfortably without showing the world my undies. However, it also made me feel quite unlike a friend and a lot more like a girlfriend. He pulled me back so I was leaning against his chest. My little heart kicked against my ribs with all the fury of a toddler in the throes of a temper tantrum. It wanted me to listen to it, to tell Daniel how I felt about him, but my brain scolded me for even considering such things.

"I have another confession. I can't dance," Daniel said, his breath warming my ear and toying with my hair.

"Honestly, Daniel, that doesn't surprise me," I said, laughing at him. "I can teach you. It's easy. You'll be a pro by prom."

"Really?"

"Sure. You get me an A in calculus, and I'll have you cuttin' a rug in no time. Rose can help, too. She's better than me, actually." I toyed with the hem of my dress, having nothing else to do with my hands.

"My mom called while you were in the bathroom. Becca's so excited about her appointment on Monday. I really hope it goes well." His subject change wasn't all that odd since I was already wondering how Becca was doing with all the stress, so I went with it.

"I hope so, too. When are they supposed to be back?"

"Monday night," he said, settling his chin on my shoulder. "Probably late."

"Want to hang out tomorrow since they'll be gone? And you're welcome to have dinner at our house if you want," I offered, trying to fill any and all silence that could pop up. Silence would give my mind and heart a chance to confuse me further about my feelings.

"Okay. Listen, Peaches, I wanted to ask you something." He lifted his head and leaned it back on the shelf. "I was wondering, if this thing with Ronin doesn't go how you want, would you maybe—"

My phone started ringing, so I pulled it from my bag. Ronin was calling. I glanced over my shoulder, and Daniel nodded. "Go ahead. I can wait."

He helped me up because I like to wander around when I talk on the phone—a habit of sorts. "Hello?" I answered.

"Hey, can we talk?" Ronin's voice sounded a little strained, annoyed even.

"Sure, but I thought you were calling tomorrow?" I asked, running my finger along one dusty shelf. I spotted a book I wanted to buy, so I slid it out and tucked it under my arm as I walked.

"Yeah, I don't think this can wait. This has all gone too far," Ronin said.

"What's gone too far?" I stopped at the end of the aisle, confused.

"Sara told me what you did, Hazel. It's not funny, and I would never have thought you'd do something so mean. It's just not like you. At least, I didn't think it was until today," he said.

What did I do? I thought back over our interaction in the bathroom and couldn't come up with a single thing I'd done that could be considered mean. In fact, it was quite the opposite. I'd tried to bite my tongue when all I wanted to do was smack her. "What are you talking about? What did she say I did?"

"Attacking her in the bathroom? Screaming at her to stay away from me?" he said, his tone very angry. "I know you guys aren't friends, but you can at least be civil to one another."

"Ronin, I didn't do that! She was the one who—"

"Then paying that girl to spill slushy on her head. That was just low, Hazel. Forget about talking tomorrow. I'm so over this craziness."

Wow, how Sara could spin the truth. But Ronin should have known I would never behave that way. Sure, I thought what Natalie did was funny, but I would never ask someone to do that.

"Ronin, I did no such thing! Sara was the one who yelled at me. As for the slushy, she earned that all on her own. Maybe she should be nicer to people, and they wouldn't want to drown her with her own drink!"

"I had to listen to her complaining the whole way back to her place, Hazel. We broke up, deal with it, okay? Just move on and stop attacking my friends," he spat.

"I am dealing with it. You're the one who asked me to talk, Ronin. What else do you want me to do? She attacked me, and if you think I'm lying, then you don't know me at all." My voice cracked. Tears started to sting my eyes again. I walked around to the next aisle, so Daniel wouldn't see them.

"I thought I did. I thought I knew you better than anyone. What happened?" Ronin asked, his voice suddenly much calmer than before.

"You decided I wasn't good enough for you anymore. That's what happened. I didn't change, Ronin. You did." Silence filled the line, and I thought he hung up until he sighed.

"I'm sorry. You're right. Sara is a lunatic," his voice was sincere, but I wasn't so sure I cared. "She's driving me crazy, always talking about all the things you did wrong."

"Well, you're dating her, so what does that say about you?" I asked coldly.

"Whoa, I'm not dating her. Oh no, she annoys the snot out of me. Tanner is into her, so he begged me to let her hang around for a while," he admitted.

"Tanner has a girlfriend. You know what, I don't care. Good luck with the love triangle... square... whatever love shape thingy you've got there. I'm over it too."

"I know you are. You moved on pretty fast for someone who supposedly loved me," Ronin said, hitting low. However, from his point of view, that was what I did. "One minute you wanted us back together, the next you were kissing some guy. It was literally the same day we broke up, not even an hour later, Hazel."

"That was... I..."

"Were you cheating on me? With *him?*" he asked.

"What? No! I wasn't—"

"Forget it. I did want to talk to you about getting back together, but this whole thing is too much. I can't take the drama anymore." His tone was stressed, and he sounded like he was ready to puke.

"So, when you said you loved me, was it a lie?" I asked, afraid to know the answer no matter what it was, but I needed to know so I could find a way to move on.

"No, I loved you. I still do," he said, "But it's not enough."

"What more do you want?" I asked, tears slipping from my eyes. One would think being dumped publicly, humiliated beyond belief, and losing your best friend would be the worst pain you could imagine, but I was wrong. Hearing someone tell you they loved you, but it wasn't enough—that was the worst pain imaginable.

"Hazel, we just don't work. I miss you, but I'll get over it, and so will you." His voice was sorrowful, making me wish he'd kept up his jerkiness. Maybe it wouldn't have hurt as much if he'd had a nasty tone rather than one that sounded as miserable as I felt.

"I'm gonna hang up now, Hazel. I think it's better if we don't talk anymore, okay? Tee really likes you, and I'm fine with sharing friends, but we should probably steer clear of each other for a while. It's for the best, in the end, you'll see." With that, he hung up the phone, shutting me out of his life forever. We wouldn't be together. We wouldn't even be friends.

I loved him, but it wasn't enough. I wasn't enough.

It felt like an elephant sat on my chest, squashing me until I couldn't breathe. It was so final, so over. At least before, I had hope. Now even that was gone.

"Peaches?" Daniel's voice pulled me back. I was on the floor, sitting in a crying heap of Hazel. "What did he do to you?"

Daniel was angry, but it was fleeting. He scooped me up and stood me on my own two feet. I leaned on him, but he made me stand upright. Every time I tried to use him as support, he made me support myself. It felt awfully mean, especially since all I wanted was his comforting embrace. It's what a real best friend would have done. A real best friend would have coddled me and told me I was pretty until I felt better, but not Daniel. He wouldn't let me. He did wipe a few stray tears from my face before looking me in the eyes.

"I care about you enough to make you do this on your own, Peaches. You're strong enough; you don't need to lean on me. I'm here. I always will be here, but you're standing on your own two feet because you can."

I stared at him, feeling lost and confused, but also something else. "I'm not good enough."

"For him?"

"For anyone."

His anger returned, but again, it was only fleeting.

"Wait here." He walked away for a moment and returned with the giant stuffed bear. "Here, take this."

"Why?" I asked, wiping tears.

"Just take it, please. Here, take its hands." He shoved the bear's hands into mine and began swaying it back and forth.

"What are you doing besides making me look like a fool on top of being miserable?" I asked, sniffling.

"This old man bear, he sits on that chair all day, every day. He probably wants to gouge his eyeballs out or plug his ears just to get away from the monotony of his day, but guess what? Today was different. Today, the old man bear got to dance with a beautiful girl. You did that, Peaches. You made this bear happy today."

He dropped the bear to the side and took my hands, swaying to nonexistent music. "Teach me to dance, Peaches. Be here with me and forget about Ronin and his insecurities because they aren't yours."

"The store closes in fifteen minutes, Daniel."

"Better get to work then, huh?" he asked, still swaying like a ten-year-old at his first dance.

"Fine, come here, dork."

For fifteen minutes, I taught Daniel how to dance, and for fifteen minutes, I forgot about everything that worried me. I didn't need Ronin to make me feel good about myself. I didn't need *anyone* to make me feel good about myself. Daniel was right. I could do it on my own. I certainly *could,* but it was sure nice knowing I had Daniel in my corner, too.

"Closing time, guys." The lady from the check-out counter in the café—cranky old woman—smiled at us when she informed us of the time. "You two are so sweet."

Daniel and I both cocked our heads to the side. "Huh. I thought she hated us," he said.

"Me, too."

"Maybe our combined adorableness wore her down?" he asked.

"Beats me, but Daniel?" I tugged on his hand when he tried to release me. While we were dancing, I made a choice. New deal. I didn't want Ronin back, but I did want revenge for my broken heart.

"What is it, Peaches?"

"I want to ruin Ronin McKinsey," I said, then waited for some long, drawn-out speech about why it was a bad idea, never expecting his response.

"Now that, Peaches, I can do."

Ten

D aniel did a fantastic job of cheering me up, but as soon as he was out of sight, I felt lonely and miserable again. Normally after a break-up, my friends would surround me with happiness until I recovered and moved on. Unfortunately, none of my previous boyfriends were Ronin, and now all my friends were gone, thanks to Sara. Though, they probably weren't the greatest friends in the first place if they jumped ship so quickly—all but Tee, of course.

I made it home before Rose, which meant Dizzy spent the better part of the night trying to convince me that Daniel *was* an option. I nodded my agreement, but deep down, I knew I could never keep up with him. He'd grow bored of lackluster conversation with someone like me, a far less intelligent human being with a severe addiction to going overboard.

By morning, I was comfortable with my position. Daniel's best friend forever and always. Or so I told myself.

"You're up early, dear." My father was sitting at the kitchen table, drinking a cup of coffee, but it wouldn't keep him awake. His double shift at the hospital wore him down, and I knew the second he hit the bed, he'd be out for ten hours—the life of an ER doctor, but he loved it.

"I have plans for most of the day," I said, offering him a bowl of cereal as I prepared my own.

"No, thanks. I'm heading to bed soon. I wanted to ask, how are you doing?" He put his coffee down and gave me his full focus.

"Fine, really. It is what it is. Shake it off, right?" I asked.

"I know these things aren't easy, but I promise it won't suck so much in a few weeks. I've been there myself more than once, and I remember it all too well." He smiled. He was so tired but tried very hard to stay awake in case I needed to talk. He was a great father, always had been even if the job pulled him away from us more often than we liked.

"I know, Dad. You need some rest, but I'll be home for dinner. We can catch up then." I assured him, then urged him to bed. He hugged me and started toward the master bedroom, shuffling his feet as he went.

"Oh, one more thing, if your Mom asks—"

"I know. We had a long and meaningful conversation about boys." I rolled my eyes, and Dad gave me a thumbs up. Neither of us was ever keen on sharing our deepest feelings with one another, yet my mother insisted we do so anyway. Our long-standing agreement was to pretend we did for our mother's sake. Oddly enough, we seemed to connect much better with a few sentences than we ever would if we had a full heart-to-heart.

"Hey, Daddy," Rose said as she passed him on her way to the kitchen. I heard Dizzy greet him as well, and both appeared at the table, ready to drill me about my night with Daniel and our plans for the day.

"Nothing," I said before they even had a chance. "Nothing happened. Nothing will ever happen. We are just friends, so deal with it."

"Whoa, look who woke up on the cranky side of the bed this morning," Dizzy said. She held her hands up in mock defense. "I said all I had to say last night. Now it's up to you to run with it. Which you should do. Which you should definitely, definitely do."

"Look, he's a great guy, yeah, but we're not a couple. That's not going to change. I like having him as a friend, and I won't risk losing that, especially on a rebound."

Rose fiddled with her napkin while Dizzy made toast. "That's fair, I guess. Sorry, we won't push anymore. I know the whole thing's been crazy, but I really just want you to be happy. Daniel makes you happy, so... I guess it made sense in my head," Rose said.

"He doesn't have to be my boyfriend to make me happy, Rose," I reminded, but even as I said it, I flinched internally. It was true. He certainly could make me happy as a friend, but I wanted more than that. I swallowed the lump of anxiety that grew bigger by the moment and picked up my bowl to finish off the milk.

"You're right. And if he makes you happy as a friend, then I'm happy, too," Rose said.

"Thank you. It has been crazy, which is why I just need to clear my head for a while. By the way, the new plan. I don't want to get back together with Ronin, but I am going to make him regret the day he humiliated me in front of half the school," I said, wiping milk from my face.

"What are you planning, Hazel?" Rose asked, cocking her head to give me a side-eyed warning—don't go nuts.

"Nothing much, just making him squirm a little before moving on. By the way, I need ideas for Daniel's prom date. Seriously, I have no idea anymore," I said.

"Why not you? You can go as friends, right?" Dizzy suggested.

"I think he wants a real date." I dropped my bowl in the sink and leaned against the counter. "We're spending the day together. Want to join?"

I had four real friends in the world, and half of them were standing in the room with me. I seriously doubted it would take Daniel and me all day to come up with a few torturous things to do to Daniel—and Sara while we were at it—so I didn't see any harm in all of us hanging out for a few hours.

"I was doing something with Tee tonight, but I think we're both free until then," Rose said.

Dizzy sighed. "I see how it is. Get a brand-new boyfriend and ditch the bestie." She swiped at a fake tear and dramatically fell into the seat beside Rose. Rose ignored her, which was sometimes the only thing you could do when it came to Dizzy. I checked my watch, noticing I had about five minutes to kill before Daniel showed up. His punctuality was somewhat annoying, especially since I had a bad habit of running behind.

"I'm gonna go get dressed before he gets here, but think of some things to do today besides sitting around staring at each other, please!" I yelled behind me as I headed toward my bedroom. I glanced at my phone, a habit, and noticed I had a missed text message. I swiped the screen and scrolled to the new message. It was from Ronin. I had a mini-crisis as I tried to figure out what to do. I almost deleted it without reading it, but I decided to read it just in case... In case of *what*, who knew. Maybe I hoped his head had exploded, and he needed someone to identify the rest of his stupid face.

Ronin

> *Sorry about last night. I was out of line accusing you. I*
> *should have known better. I was awake half the night*
> *thinking about it, and I am so sorry, Hazel.*

The last time I checked, Ronin was the one who said we
shouldn't speak again. So far, I'd held up my end of the bargain
by plotting his death instead of what I'd say to him when I saw
him next. When every fiber of my being wanted to send him a
nasty text message the night before, I controlled myself so that
I wouldn't appear to be the weaker person, the childish one.
He made it impossible to ignore him, though, which caused my
maturity to plummet to nothingness. I really wanted to send that
nasty message, but I had finally moved into the second stage
of post-break-up grief, wanting revenge, and I had no plans to
move back to step one.

I put my phone down, resisting the urge once more. It dinged
again, frustrating me further. *Please be from Daniel,* I thought.
Please be from anyone else, I prayed.

Ronin

> *I told Sara off. I told her I didn't want her to hang*
> *around me anymore, that I didn't want to date her…*
> *everything. Watch your back. She's on the warpath*
> *and blames you. I'm sorry.*

Wonderful. Not only was Ronin going back on his own
statement by texting me, but he'd also sent my demon-spawn
ex-friend to the brink of total devastation. Her target—my life.
That I could not ignore. I did nothing wrong, and I would not
let the two of them continue to ruin my senior year, especially
when I'd already made it my mission to destroy theirs. I typed a
short response.

> *Perfect. Thanks for making my life even more difficult.*

Not two seconds later, he responded.

> I'm sorry. I didn't know she would freak out and blame you.

> How could you not anticipate that? Of course, she would blame me!

> I was so mad I didn't think it through. This is more drama than I ever anticipated.

> You created it, Ronin. You treated me like crap, then led her to believe she had a chance with you. You made the bed. Now go sleep in it, jerk.

> Is this what we are now?

What was he talking about? There was no *we* anymore. He was the one that made that excruciatingly clear in a very public way. I put the phone down, resisting the part of me that wanted to argue with him. I had plans for the day, and they didn't involve getting into an argument with Ronin. The doorbell rang, and I heard Rose let Daniel in. If I was gonna argue with someone, Daniel was a much better person to do that with. Banter with him was fun. Fights with Ronin... not so much.

I heard stomping, and soon my door flew open, and Daniel fell onto my bed with a smile. "Good morning, Peaches!"

"What if I'd been changing, Daniel? Don't you know how to knock?" I asked.

"Sure, I do, but what fun would that be?" he asked.

"The kind where you don't see me naked!"

"I fail to see how that is remotely fun, Peaches," he said in an excellent mood so early in the morning. I was glad one of us was. Maybe his attitude would wear off on me, and I could wipe the memory of Ronin's early morning messages from my mind.

"It would be embarrassing for me, and you think that's fun? I thought you were my best friend?" Rose and Dizzy found their way to my room, lounging on the floor, listening to us fuss.

"Hmm, that's a tough one. On the one hand, I'd probably feel crummy for embarrassing you, but on the other... naked hot girl." He balanced his hands in front of him like a set of scales, a weighted decision to make. Rose gave him a disapproving look, and he caved. "Fine, I'll start knocking."

"And?" Rose asked.

"And I will never make inappropriate jokes again. Sorry," Daniel said.

Dizzy started in with her splat ball again. She tossed it up and waited for it to peel and fall from the ceiling. Daniel watched her do it with intense focus, especially considering it was literally a squishy, sticky ball whose only purpose was to make a splat noise. Rose stared at the ceiling, probably daydreaming about Tee, while I watched the three of them doing absolutely nothing with their day.

If there was anything I hated more than backstabbing best friends and stupid ex-boyfriends, it was a wasted day. "Oh, come on! This thing can't be that much fun!" I fussed.

Not one of them paid a bit of attention to me, but they were awfully interested in the multiple dings from my phone. Daniel grabbed it from my nightstand before I could reach it. He started to hand it to me, but when he saw who they were from, he snatched it back. His eyes narrowed, and his jaw clenched tightly as he scrolled through them.

"Daniel, can I have my phone, please?" I asked, a little annoyed he was going through the messages without my consent. Rose and Dizzy were quiet, neither daring to get into the middle of whatever was about to go down. Daniel handed me the phone, and I discovered the source of his anger. Dozens of messages spammed my phone. All from Sara, and all less than kind. Many were jabs at my personality, some were attacks on my relationship with Daniel, but most were vicious threats to stay away from Ronin.

"This has gone on long enough, Peaches," Daniel said, calming enough to speak.

Rose reached for the phone, so I let her take it. She and Dizzy read through the messages with wide eyes and gaping mouths. "What a... a... You know, I can't think of a word nasty enough to describe her," Dizzy said, pointing to the phone.

"Guys, it's not a big deal. I was expecting it, actually," I said, surprised to find that I actually didn't care. The messages didn't bother me. I just... didn't care anymore.

"Not a big deal?" Rose shouted, then remembered our father was trying to sleep. If we weren't quiet, our mother would send us all away for the afternoon.

"Shh... Look, Ronin sent me a few messages this morning." I showed her the messages he sent. "Honestly, I don't care. She'll get over herself soon enough."

Dizzy snickered. "Well, that's very mature of you, considering she called you that word you really, really hate."

"Wait, she did?" I looked over the messages again. "Oh, look there, she did it twice. What a potty mouth," I said.

"You really don't care, Peaches?" Daniel asked. I shook my head, and that was enough for him. "Okay, then, moving on to fun stuff. What are we doing—" The dinging interrupted his sentence, sparking that fire again. I looked at the phone to see it was Ronin with more apologies.

"You know what? Why don't I turn this off?" I powered the phone down and tossed it in my dresser drawer. "Who's up for a trip to the zoo?"

I surprised everyone and shocked them right into silence. It was a little surprising, what with my penchant for doing everything I could to make sure everyone liked me, obsessing over every detail of everything that ever happened as much as possible, and my constant need to make things right. The old me would have worked overtime to please Ronin, but the me who like Daniel... Well, she didn't care all that much.

"The zoo? Sara attacked you, and you want to go to the zoo?" Dizzy asked, her splat ball dangerously close to falling on her face if she didn't pay attention to it.

"Sure. It's nothing some cotton candy and cuddly animals can't fix." When no one moved, I said, "Guys, please. Let's go before I start to overanalyze this and go bonkers trying to defend myself from two losers."

It was coming. I felt it. My resolve was only so firm. I was in real danger of jerking open my dresser drawer and telling Sara precisely what I thought about her if I didn't get out of the room. It would only be satisfying for a minute, then I would feel like a foolish child, duped into stooping to her level.

Rose jumped up first. "I could do cotton candy at nine in the morning."

"Me, too," Dizzy said, catching the ball at the last second.

Daniel slid off the bed and took my hand. "Okay, Peaches, if that's what you really want, that's what we'll do. Besides, while we're there, we can see some of Sara's relatives."

Dizzy laughed, but the joke was lost on me.

"What? I don't get it," I said.

"The poo-slinging monkeys, Peaches. The dirty, dirty, backstabbing, poo-slinging monkeys," he said.

I arched my eyebrow, wondering if that was supposed to be funny or if he and Dizzy just had similar enough IQs that they understood something Rose and I did not. My sister looked at me with a furrowed brow and a confused expression. I was beginning to feel stupid when Dizzy spoke.

"That was the worst joke I've ever heard," she said and shook her head.

"Give me time. I'll come up with something better," Daniel said, following her down the hall.

"Doubtful," she teased.

"You're so negative."

"You're so weird."

"I'm weird? How am I... Okay, fine. But Peaches likes me just how I am so, thhhhbbbb!" He gave her a raspberry, very childish, yet exactly what I needed to solidify my good mood again.

"Daniel's driving!" I yelled, passing them in a hurry to get shotgun in my own car.

"No! I want a ride on the bike!" Dizzy yelled. I'd almost forgotten about the death trap Daniel liked to whiz around on. He looked at me, gauging my reaction. I slipped on my shoes and pulled my hair into a ponytail.

"Fine," I said. "I'll drive with Rose, but be careful! He's a lunatic on that thing, I swear."

Dizzy jumped around, excited as can be. The two were out the door and halfway down the street before Rose and I even had our seatbelts clicked into place. It was all the same; I wanted to hear about my sister's date anyway.

While we drove, I got her up to speed with the whole Natalie and Sara slushy incident and what Ronin did while Daniel and I were at the library. I wanted to tell her about my feelings for Daniel and why I thought we would never work, but ultimately decided there was no point. I'd already decided we would only be friends, and I would never share the secret about his intelligence with anyone, not even my sister.

We hit every red light on the way, got stuck behind an accident, and lost in a sea of cars in the parking lot of the zoo. Finally, we found Daniel and Dizzy already halfway finished with their cotton candy, sitting just outside of the big cat sanctuary.

"Where have you guys been?" Dizzy asked. We waited around out front, but we got hungry.

"Traffic, life, whatever. Give me some of that." Rose snatched the candy from Dizzy's hand, forcing a sour look on her friend's face when she lost her sugary treat.

Daniel handed me his with no questions asked. He took my hand, and we wandered down the path to the tiger enclosure. Rose and Dizzy traded jokes behind us, and it was all a lot of fun and games until someone got hurt, namely me—again. The enclosure had a low-hanging sign, which was rather stupid, all things considered, and I caught the corner of it with my eye.

"Peaches, you're a one-woman walking disaster, did you know that?" Daniel teased, but his concern was written all over his face.

He wasn't wrong about the status of my clumsiness, but we had to go to the medical center inside the zoo, nonetheless. A lovely nurse, also named Rose, gave me a butterfly bandage and an ice pack, then filled out an incident report. This time I agreed to it. That sign bit me and needed to be put down! She assured me I was not the first to have an unpleasant meeting with it, and she would make sure it was removed as soon as possible.

By the time that was all said and done, my stomach growled. Lunch called my name, so we found ourselves eating anything and everything we could get our hands on as we walked through the rest of the zoo. It was pleasant, spending time with friends and sharing everything with them. My former friends wouldn't let me steal so much as a potato chip from their plates. Rose tossed a chicken nugget to me before taking half my soft pretzel, but Dizzy simply sat with her hot dog, nibbling at it, deep in concentration.

Daniel nudged her, gaining her attention. She looked at him with a fearful expression, one that I'd never seen on her face before, and it worried me. Dizzy wasn't afraid of anything. She was the one who helped the people around her overcome fear, not the one who showed it.

"What's wrong?" Rose asked her best friend.

"Um..." Dizzy put her hot dog down and wiped her fingers on her napkin, looking at Daniel again. He nodded encouragingly, but she continued to stare.

"Just tell them, Diz. They're going to understand, I promise," he said.

"I know. I want to, it's just a lot harder than I thought it would be to talk about it," she said. There was a secret the two shared, and I found myself a little jealous for absolutely no reason.

"Just spit it out super-fast, and before you know it, we'll be moving on to something else. They love you, no matter what. This doesn't change anything." Daniel put his own food down and turned in his seat to face her. "Go on, you can do it. You've needed to get this out, and now's your chance. I promise you, you're making a bigger deal of this than it is."

Dizzy inhaled and looked back at Rose and me. "I'm adopted, and I went to meet my birth mother last week. I have three other siblings I never knew about, and I think I want to get to know them, so I might be spending the summer four hours away," she spat in a super-fast run-on sentence like Daniel suggested.

Rose looked at me, and I looked at her, both blinking a few times. Once we were sure we both heard correctly, Rose turned back to Dizzy and said, "And? Were you anxious about telling us that?"

"You don't think it's weird?" Dizzy asked.

"I have loads of questions, starting with how on earth did you discover you are adopted, but mostly I just want to support my best friend. You are my best friend, right?" Rose asked.

"Of course. I just... I didn't know how to talk about it. Your family has always been amazing, not like mine. And then I found out I was adopted and... I guess I'm just feeling all over the place right now," Dizzy said.

"Hey, I know it hasn't been easy at home. I'm here, and if you need to talk, then you know I'll listen," Rose said. "I try not to bring things up unless you want to talk."

Dizzy exhaled slowly, the weight of her secret finally off her shoulders. I couldn't imagine how she felt. Her home life had always been rough, the reason she spent most of her time at ours.

"Hazel?" she asked. "Wh-what do you think?"

I didn't even hesitate. There were a lot of people in my life that confused me, but never Dizzy. "I think you are an amazing person, and if you want to form a bond with your biological family, then I think that's wonderful. I'm here, too," I said.

She breathed another sigh of relief. "Oh, thank goodness. You have no idea how long I've been trying to get that out. Every time I tried to bring it up, I choked on the words. It seems a little silly now, but... I don't know. I'm already feeling rejected by my adoptive family, and it's weird to know I have this whole other family that wants to get to know me."

Rose smiled, then put up a finger. "I can understand that, but one question. How does Daniel find out before me, your best friend?"

Dizzy glanced at Daniel with a little shrug. "I was afraid to talk about it, so I asked his advice."

"You told a total stranger before you told me?" Rose laughed.

"What can I say? He's super easy to talk to." Dizzy joined Rose in her laughter, all the while I watched Daniel.

Her statement could not have been more accurate. Daniel was perhaps the best person in the world to spill your guts to. He didn't judge, well, not too much, at least. His advice was usually reliable, and he genuinely cared about the people in his life—demonstrated by his reaction to Sara's bullying and Dizzy's secret.

I wished things were different. I wished I were somewhere close to his level of intelligence, not that I was stupid, but I would never measure up to the kind of people that would surround him at his internship. He would go on to his new life, find some super brainy genius woman he could have long, intelligent conversations with, and I, Hazel Simmons, would probably be left behind, still trying to figure out what to do with my life.

Friends, Hazel. A friend is all you can ever hope to be to Daniel Starnes.

Eleven

"Lauren Hart."

"She's a sophomore, Peaches," Daniel said, turning down the fifth name I came up with in an hour. He'd given me every excuse in the book. Too tall, too short, too loud, too quiet, and now—too young. I was starting to think he didn't really want to go to prom since most of his responses were not accurate and delivered with a guilty smirk.

"Daniel, I'm never going to find you a date to prom if you don't give me something to work with," I complained. I settled back and rested my head on the old man bear, which was propped against Daniel's lap. The associates at the bookstore had accepted that we were permanent fixtures, and if we bought coffee or some other item at least once, they didn't care. Even the cranky old lady didn't mind us anymore, but I was pretty sure that was thanks to my arranging books on the shelves, so she didn't have to.

"I don't know," he said, running his fingers through my hair. I was pretty sure he was getting cookie crumbs in it, too, but it felt too good to make him stop. He leaned against the bookcase munching on his giant sugar cookie.

"If you don't know, how can I know?" I asked. "Oh, maybe... No, never mind. She just started dating that Peter guy who kinda looks a little bit like you."

"Too bad, so sad." Daniel finished off the cookie and wiped his hands on his pants. "Want to go back to my house and binge-watch something?"

"What's wrong with sitting here talking?"

"All you're doing is shouting random names at me. How is that talking?" he asked. He sat forward and made me sit up.

"Aww, I was comfortable," I whined.

"You'll be more comfortable on my couch. Come on, Peaches. We'll get some ice cream on the way." He pulled me into a standing position against my will, waved to cranky old lady, and pushed me out the door.

The little bell over the door at Fire and Ice dinged, but this time it didn't make my heart crack. This time, all I wanted was ice cream. Unfortunately, so did Ronin, and he turned around to see who walked in just as we shut the door. Daniel ignored him entirely and walked up to the counter, ordering his favorite and mine without hesitation.

I felt Ronin staring at me, but I wouldn't give him the satisfaction of acknowledging his existence. Instead, I slipped my hand into Daniel's and shimmied a little closer. He shook his hand free and wrapped his arm around my shoulders, tucking me nicely against his chest instead. I didn't realize how chilly it was in the shop until I was pressed against him, warm and snuggly. He handed me my ice cream and left a tip in the jar. We were almost out the door, ready to get on with our day... *almost*.

"Hey, Hazel." Ronin's voice was strained but loud enough that I couldn't play off like I didn't hear him. I turned around to find him standing right beside me.

"Oh, hi," I said. I let Daniel wrap both arms around my waist and pull me against his chest a little tighter. I'm not sure why we continued the charade since I was no longer trying to make Ronin jealous, but we did, and the look on Ronin's face was priceless.

"I tried to call you earlier, but I guess you were busy," he said, choosing not to look at Daniel, probably to avoid the smirk I was sure was plastered on Daniel's face.

"Oh, yeah, Daniel and I were at the zoo with Rose and Dizzy. I left my phone at home because your girlfriend was blowing it up with hate mail," I replied with a little too much sarcasm.

"I told you, she's not my girlfriend. Never was," Ronin said.

"Babe, I'm gonna go get the bike while you finish your ice cream, okay?" Daniel allowed me to handle things on my own, and I appreciated it immensely. It meant he had faith in me, he believed I could hold my own against my adversary and come out on top. And Ronin, he was the worst kind of adversary. The kind who pretended to love you then went and broke you into a million pieces—repeatedly.

"Sure, I won't be long," I said.

Daniel started to walk out but turned at the last second. For a moment, I thought maybe he'd changed his mind. Maybe he didn't believe I could do it, but that wasn't the case. He simply wanted to get his own jab in at my ex before walking out.

He slid his hand around my waist and bent down, his lips landing gently on mine. I hadn't expected it, so I was a little stiff, but soon melted the way I always did when Daniel kissed me. If that was how it felt to kiss him when no feelings were involved, I couldn't imagine what it would feel like if he liked me as more than a friend. Ronin cleared his throat, a clear signal he was uncomfortable, but I ignored him.

Once Daniel decided he'd made his point, he handed me his helmet. "I need to buy another helmet since this is a permanent thing, you and me." He looked back at Ronin, who was thoroughly disgusted. "Nice seeing you again, Roger."

"Ronin," I corrected.

"Are you sure? I thought it was Roger. Oh well. Nice seeing you, Robert!"

I took the helmet and smiled at Daniel before urging him to go. He took one last look before heading down the block to get the bike, a wide smirk on his face. He was pleased with himself, and it made me smile.

"Are you actually dating him?" Ronin asked.

"Is it any of your business what I do?" I asked. "You broke up with me, which means I get to do what I want without worrying about what you think." I started to walk away, not at all in the mood to let him ruin my day.

"You're right. I'm sorry, Hazel. This is all new territory, okay?" he pleaded.

"It's what you wanted, Ronin. And I think you were right. I think we should stop speaking to each other. You've already got Sara after me, so please, let's not make this any worse than it already is," I said.

"I shouldn't have said that. I was—"

"Ronin, please. You keep saying stupid things to me, then you turn around and say you shouldn't have. That excuse is old, it's tired, and I'm over it," I interrupted.

"We were friends for a long time, Hazel, and now you're just gone. It's a little strange and... I know I screwed up, okay?" His loud voice got us some unwanted attention, so he urged me to go outside. I pushed open the front door and huffed out, annoyed he wouldn't just go away. Once we were out of the view of nosey ice cream patrons, he continued. "We had a great thing for a long time, and maybe if I had been honest with you, it wouldn't have gotten so out of hand. I'm sorry about that, I really am. I miss you so much."

"Gotten out of hand? What, Ronin? Me, or your inability to communicate your feelings appropriately?" I snapped.

"I... The things...You know, if I'd told you earlier how they embarrassed me, then maybe you would have stopped. You have to admit, some of the things you did were crazy," he argued.

"Maybe so, but you didn't have to react the way you did. Furthermore, some people like the way I am and wouldn't change a thing about me," I said, remembering what Daniel had told me days earlier.

"I doubt there is anyone on the planet that would appreciate being embarrassed by their girlfriend that many times and on that grand a scale, Hazel, not even Mr. Perfect." Ronin was frustrated, and I knew if I didn't get away from him, words would pass between the two of us we would *both* wish we hadn't said.

Mr. Perfect had perfect timing and came to a stop along the sidewalk beside us. Ronin glared at him as if somehow Daniel was the reason his life was spiraling out of control, then he scoffed at the bike.

"Is there something you want to say?" Daniel asked.

"Nope, just wondering how you can afford such an expensive bike," Ronin said with a judgmental tone.

"I sell crack downtown five nights a week. Ready, Peaches?"

Ronin's jaw dropped. He knew it wasn't true, but he hated that he couldn't get to Daniel through jabs and insults. I slipped on the helmet and got on the back, wrapped my arms tight around his waist, and shimmied closer. We were off, leaving Ronin behind to figure out life on his own.

It is impossible to carry a conversation when one is holding on for dear life, the wind whistling in your ears as you fly down the interstate, so when we finally made it back to Daniel's house, I had a whole load of things I wanted to say—beginning with an apology.

"I'm sorry you keep getting dragged into my drama, and I have yet to find you a date to prom for your trouble," I said as I placed the helmet on the kitchen table. He ran his hands through his hair, a sad attempt at taming the wind-blown locks. "I need to get my own helmet. It's not safe for you to ride without one."

"I already ordered one, Peaches. It'll be here in a few days, no worries." He opened the fridge and tossed me a bottle of apple juice. "Snacks?"

"I'm stuffed, thanks."

He grabbed himself a bag of pretzels, and we headed toward the living room to choose a show to binge-watch for what little of the day was left. The light was already beginning to fade, casting long shadows on the living room floor.

"How do you afford the bike, though? You have some high-paying job I don't know about?" I joked but really was curious.

He laughed. "My grandparents bought it for me. They feel bad that they raised a horrible son who ran out on his family, so they buy my love with motorcycles and trust funds. They even bought my mom her car—both of them."

"So, no crack then?" I asked, making him laugh even harder.

"Sorry to disappoint, Peaches, but no, no crack. Ronin is a jerk, by the way. A *stupid* jerk. He's used to getting his way, isn't he?" he asked.

"Yeah, basically. Sorry, again, it's not fair you keep—"

"Want to go to prom with me?" he blurted, standing in front of me with a remote control in one hand, pretzels in the other, and a blank stare.

"Um..." *Yes,* my head screamed, yes! But my mouth wouldn't let me say the word since it wasn't entirely sure of the reason he asked me to go.

He noted my hesitation and backpedaled a little. "I was just thinking, there's really no one at school I like enough to ask, and since you're not going with Ronin... Okay, it was a stupid idea. Never mind."

"No!" I shouted and grabbed his arm. I took a breath and reigned myself in before I behaved like a total desperate nutcase. "I mean, no, it's fine. I'd like to go with you... as friends, right?"

"Yeah, as friends. Takes the pressure off, right?"

"Yeah, right. No pressure, just friends."

"So, two friends going to prom together. It could be fun, yeah?" he asked with a nervous glance at the television before looking back at me. Was he trying to convince himself or me? I'd already said yes, but I was beginning to think he wanted me to say no.

"Sure? I mean, we have a lot of fun together. Besides, I think everyone probably expects us to go together anyway since..." *Way to go, Hazel.* I had to go and rub it in that he basically *had* to go to prom with me since everyone already thought we were dating. That, or stage a break-up.

"Yeah, I mean, I thought that too. People think we're dating, so it would throw off the whole plan if we went with other people, right?" he asked, only making me feel worse.

My shoulders slumped, and I sighed. I really wanted to go with him, but not like that. I didn't want to force him to go with me for a stupid plan.

"I'm sorry, Daniel. We can stage a break-up if you'd rather go with someone else," I said, but deep down, I prayed he truly wanted to go with me.

"Is that what you want?" He stood stock-still, that silly blinking remote still in one hand and bag of pretzels in the other. The last rays of sunlight shone through the curtains and toyed with his russet locks, making them appear a deeper shade of red. The hazel eyes staring back at me were deep gold, the color of honey, yet with the slightest tinge of green—an odd thing to notice from so far away. And that's when I realized I'd somehow migrated closer to him, practically on top of the poor guy. He would have to physically move me to sit on his sofa.

He had me so turned around I didn't even have control over my own body anymore.

"I um... I don't know. I mean, is it what you want to do?" I asked.

He studied me for a moment, his gold and moss-colored eyes doing their best to read me. "I want you to be happy. I want you to have a good time at prom, and I think maybe I can help you with both."

"Both?" I whispered, suddenly feeling a little claustrophobic with his eyes boring down on me the way they were.

"I think if we went to prom together, I could make you happy, and we'd have a good time. As friends, I mean," he added as an afterthought.

I nodded. "Okay. I think so, too."

"So, it's a date then? A friends date?" he asked.

"Mmm-hmm, a friends date. I've already got a dress and everything," I said, trying to lighten the heaviness I felt in my chest every time I heard that awful word—*friend.*

"I'm sure you could wear a paper bag and look beautiful, Peaches." He dropped the pretzels on the table and stepped back, probably just as uncomfortable as I was with our closeness. I had no idea what happened, but it left me feeling confused and emotionally overwhelmed.

"What are we watching, Peaches?" he asked, his demeanor suddenly carefree and laid back again. "Maybe a comedy? I think we need to laugh our butts off the next few hours."

"Sure, sounds good to me," I said, trying to relax and enjoy our time together. There would be plenty of time to obsess over the complicated relationship we had later, like when I was alone and had nothing better to do with my time. I sat at one end of the sofa, and Daniel sat at the other, relaxed as he munched on his pretzels. He was utterly oblivious to my state of confusion.

"So, what are your plans for ruining this ex of yours?" he asked.

"I don't know. Maybe it's not such a good idea to go all bonkers. I should just move on and get over it already."

He paused the show I hadn't even begun watching yet. "Absolutely not. He has to learn his lesson, or he'll just do the same thing to the next girl he tricks into dating him."

"Daniel, it was partially my fault we broke up. He did it all wrong, but he's entitled to his feelings," I defended. As much as I hated to admit it, it was true. Ronin handled it wrong, but he couldn't control what embarrassed him, what he liked or didn't like, and how it made him feel.

"Why do you keep defending him? I thought you said you were done with him?" Daniel snapped. It took me by surprise, so I jumped a little at the sound of his raised voice.

"Daniel... I... What?"

He got up from the sofa and walked into the kitchen, leaving me sitting alone, dumbfounded. If I had gotten up and walked over to the brick fireplace, banged my head against it until I smashed my brain into goo, it would have hurt a lot less than trying to figure out teenage boys. I got up and followed Daniel into the kitchen, finding him staring into the refrigerator with a generally annoyed look on his face.

"Daniel?"

"I'm fine. I'm sorry I snapped. I just hate when you defend Ronin," he said curtly.

"I wasn't defending him. He's a giant jerk, and he's stupid, but that doesn't mean he doesn't have feelings."

"I'm sorry if I can't bring myself to care about his feelings when he's made you cry more than once."

Daniel slammed the refrigerator door closed. Something inside rattled and fell, making a splat noise when it settled. He noticed it, too, but didn't dare open the door to investigate. The look on his face was funny, and I couldn't stifle my giggle.

He looked back at me, and his irritation started to fade. Finally, his lips curved, and he broke into a smile. "I have no idea what that was," he said and laughed.

I took advantage of his happier mood and tried to explain my position. "Listen, I really appreciate everything you've done for me, Daniel. Honestly, it's been above and beyond, but I realized something at Fire and Ice today."

He pulled out a stool and sat. "What's that?"

I sat on the stool beside him and tried not to stare at his adorable face. "This thing, if I keep it going, it will never stop. I can get back at Ronin a hundred times, but all that does is keep me in the cycle, and I want out. I want to be finished with him, once and for all. Can you understand that?" I asked with a weak, questioning smile that probably looked like I needed to pee.

He studied my face again, judging my sincerity, and eventually said, "Yeah, that makes sense. I just really despise the guy, Peaches."

"Why? You didn't know him before we were friends. I mean, I appreciate best friend loyalty, but—"

"Oh, look at the time. We're gonna miss our shows."

"They're recorded, Daniel."

"Yes, but... but... Fine, I got nothing. You got me this time, Peaches. I just don't want to talk about Robert anymore."

"Ronin."

"Whatever, both names are stupid." He slid from the stool to stand beside me. "Just promise me one thing, Peaches?"

"Anything."

"Don't let Sara off so easily?"

"Oh, no. She is goin' down, no doubt about it. I just don't know how," I said, trying to get down from the stool without sliding down *him* as well. His smile grew wider, and I could tell he kept something from me.

"I'm so glad you said that. I have something to show you. Wait here." He darted off toward his bedroom. He reappeared, holding a small booklet I recognized. It was the cheer squad handbook.

"Why do you have a copy of the cheer squad handbook?" I asked.

"Because I had aspirations once, Peaches," he said sarcastically. "Because I was looking for something, and I found exactly what I was looking for."

He handed me the book with a single page dog-eared. I opened it to the page and read over the information I had never paid much attention to before. Why would I? We had never made it all the way to the regional competition before, so there was no reason to read the regulations. The more I read, the happier I got.

According to the handbook, the squad could not make any significant changes to the lineup less than sixty days before the regional competition, as per regulation. Which meant Sara could not replace me as team captain if they wanted to compete at regionals. "Please tell me you have a calendar somewhere in this house."

"I already did the math, Peaches, or I wouldn't have brought it up. Fifty-eight days. They outed you fifty-eight days before the regional competition."

"So... So, this means—"

"You're still captain, and Sara's about to have an awful Monday," he said.

"I can't believe you did this, Daniel! The thought never crossed my mind. I was just too mad!"

"What are best friends for, Peaches?" He grinned, the crooked smile I liked. I was so excited I leaped from the chair and kissed him smack bang on the mouth.

Twelve

- -

The second my lips landed on Daniel's, I wanted to murder myself. Not ten minutes after the whole going as friends to prom fiasco, I made our situation even more awkward by kissing him out of the blue. I had never wanted Ronin to pop up unexpectedly more than I did at that moment just so I could blame it on him. But alas... it was all me and my runaway mouth.

"Did... did you just kiss me, or did you trip and fall on my face?" Daniel asked, frozen in place.

"Um... yes?" I squeaked.

"Yes, you kissed me? Yes, you fell?" Still frozen except for the expression on his face that went from shocked to worried to... who knew. All I knew was that I probably looked like a giant tomato head. No one in history had ever wanted a floor to open and swallow them as much as I did.

"Yes, I kissed you," I admitted in the quietest, squeakiest voice I could mutter. Maybe if I played mousy, he would have mercy on my poor, tortured soul.

"Oh. Okay. Why exactly did you do that?"

It was impossible to discern from his stature or tone of voice whether he was okay with it or repulsed entirely, so I thought up an excuse as fast as possible and hoped it would seem more realistic once I said it out loud.

"I'm sorry. I just got excited, and my mouth got away from me." *Dear Heaven, take my soul and end the humiliation.*

"I see. So, then... Well... I guess I'm glad we cleared that up," he said, finally moving more than his lips or eyes. He shifted his weight and glanced uncomfortably at the floor.

"Yeah, all cleared up," I said. "That could have been super weird, so it's good we're such close friends, right?" *If it wasn't weird before, it certainly is after stating it, Hazel.*

"Yeah, uh, really weird. You know, if one of us had gooey feelings or something," he said, finally sitting on the stool instead of standing there like a tree.

"Oh, totally. Good thing we don't have those kinds of feelings, right?" I sat on the opposite stool, glad to have something solid beneath me since my legs were turning to jello very quickly.

"Right. Good thing."

"Super good. Yeah, so..." I fidgeted with the corner of the handbook, searching for anything to say. "Not weird, super good."

"Yep. So, how do we do this thing?" he asked.

"What thing?" I asked, confused.

"The Sara thing?"

"What Sara thing?"

"The whole *get back at Sara for being a backstabbing, poo-slinging monkey* plan?" He looked at me as if I'd gone insane, and maybe I had because all I could do was stare blankly at him, thinking about every kiss we'd shared.

"Sara? Sara... Oh, Sara. Yeah, monkey, poo... gotcha. Um..."

"Peaches, are you okay?"

"What? Oh, yeah, good. Super good. Not weird at all. Great friends. Super good." Words continued to fall out, no matter how hard I tried to shut my mouth. It was word vomit, and it was horrific.

"Did you have an aneurysm or something?" Daniel asked, leaning in to make sure I wasn't someone else entirely. "Maybe ingest a brain-eating amoeba?"

"Huh?" I asked, but my focus was on how much closer he was and how much I wanted to kiss him again. But if I did, I was sure I would not survive the humiliation.

He stood up and pulled me back into the living room, basically pushing me onto the sofa since I was fast approaching a catatonic state. I flopped on the seat cushion, which was just the jolt my brain needed to restart and snap me back to reality—for real, finally.

"Oh, no," I whined and covered my face with my hands. "I'm so sorry I kissed you. Now it's all weird, and I can't stop being weird, and you probably think I'm a total weirdo."

"I do, but to be fair, I thought that before the kiss." Daniel pried my hands from my face and laughed at me. "It was an accident. I get it. It was weird for half a second, but I'm not mad or upset about it, okay?"

"You're sure?" I asked, wishing I could just go back in time and stop myself before it happened.

"I'm sure. We have an unconventional relationship, Peaches. It's not like we haven't kissed before, and maybe that's why it just happened. Whatever it was, it's okay," he insisted, still holding my hands because he seemed to know the second he let go of them, I'd cover my face again.

"Okay."

"Okay? For real, this time, you're okay?"

I nodded. "Yeah. I'm okay."

He released my hands, and I let them rest where they fell.

"So, the Sara thing? I'm begging you to let me be there when you tell her the good news."

"I'll have to do it at lunch or right after school when I can get a meeting with Coach, but of course, you'll be there. I wouldn't dare do it without you," I said.

"I have a question, though. Do you really want to be captain again? All those girls, they're backstabbing, ungrateful brats. I think you already know you deserve better than that," he said.

"I do know, but going to regionals was my dream. Plus, it looks good on my college apps, so for those reasons, yes." I slid further into the sofa, finally feeling more relaxed. With the prom and kiss fiasco behind us, it felt like we were back to our old routine.

"Cool. Can we do it after school? Becca's appointment is in the morning, and I wanted to call at lunch to see how it went."

"I don't see why not. Now let's watch something funny and stop wasting our time talking about stupid stuff," I said, still freaking out a little inside. I wanted something to stare at besides him.

He grabbed the remote and started the show again. I'd never seen it before, but it made me laugh so hard that I almost choked on my own spit several times. We grew sleepy fast, considering our day had been long and adventurous, and his living room was quite comfortable. Somehow, we ended up in the same position we were in at the bookstore, sprawled out with my head in his lap while he played with my hair. Between the exhausting day and the gentle way he ran his fingers through my long hair, I was dead to the world by midnight... my curfew.

I was rudely awakened by a horrible beeping noise that I soon discovered was my sister blowing up my cell phone. It wasn't the first time; there were seven missed calls from her and three from

Dizzy. I tried to sit up, but a snoring boy had me pinned to the sofa with his arm. I settled for putting it on speaker.

"Hey, what's up?"

Rose dove right into the bad news. "Finally! You missed curfew, you dummy!" she yelled, jolting Daniel awake.

"One-hundred eighty-six thousand!" he screamed, sat straight up on the sofa, and accidentally rolled me onto the floor.

"Ow," I groaned when I landed on my butt.

Rose gasped. "Are you still with Daniel? What are you doing? Get home now!"

"I fell asleep watching TV. Are Mom and Dad mad?" I asked, picking myself up off the floor as I searched for my shoes.

"They don't know. I told them you went to bed early. Come to my window, and I'll lower the fire ladder, but hurry!" With that, she hung up the phone. I groaned at the thought. I'd have to climb the emergency fire ladder into her room, which meant I would probably fall to my death the second I reached her window.

"Crap, it's quarter after twelve. Sorry, Peaches." Daniel apologized as he slipped on his shoes. "Mom let the neighbor borrow one of the cars, so all I have is the bike. We're gonna have to park a few blocks out and walk to your house, or they'll hear it."

My heart jumped into my throat. It was terrible enough riding the thing during the day, but not being able to see while zipping down the road without the safety of a car surrounding me was a terrifying thought. He sensed my hesitation.

"We won't take the highway, Peaches, and I'll drive slower."

He did, and it made me so late for curfew I knew I'd be dead if my parents caught me. After we parked the bike a block away, I sent Rose a text message.

When we arrived, I saw she had already lowered the ladder. She poked her head out the window with a disapproving scowl.

"Hurry up, they're still up talking about Dad's schedule for next week." She motioned for me to hurry, waving her hands frantically.

Daniel hoisted me up to the first rung and made sure I didn't fall, but after a few rungs, I was all on my own. *Excellent time to wear flats, Hazel.* With no grip on my shoes, my feet kept slipping on the rungs. The shoes were absolutely useless pieces of junk. I held tight to the ladder with one hand and reached back to remove them. I tried to toss one up to Rose, but I'm no pitcher, so I missed the window by several feet.

"Ow!" Daniel cried when the first shoe smacked him on the head. He caught the second, also a miss when thrown to Rose. "I'll just uh... give these to you tomorrow?" He didn't wait for a reply; he just stuffed them in his back pocket and steadied the ladder again.

I had a much better grip with bare feet, but the chain ladder was so wobbly I lost my balance anyway. As I anticipated, I fell when I was only two feet from the windowsill. I squealed all the way down, but as always, Daniel was there for me. He caught me, and we both went down together. It still hurt, but he broke my fall enough that my arms, legs, neck, and every other breakable thing were still intact when we both got up.

I heard clapping and glanced up at Rose, thinking her clapping was a little rude, considering I could have died, but her hands were still and gripping her windowsill tightly. *Oh, no.* I lowered my eyes to the window below Rose's, the dining room. Both parents were standing at the open window, clapping at us with smirks on their faces.

"I'm a dead man. See ya, Peaches!" Daniel darted off toward his bike, but my father yelled out the open window after him.

"Stop right there, young man!" Daniel froze and looked over his shoulder. "What you do right now tells me a lot about who you are as a man and as my daughter's friend. Run away like a coward or come inside and face the music." My father issued the ultimatum and walked away from the window.

My mother raised her hands in the air and shrugged with a sympathetic smile. "Good luck, kids," she said, then headed toward the stairs, likely to bed. I looked back to Daniel, still frozen in the yard with a choice to make. He grumbled and turned around, head hung, and walked toward the front door.

Rose disappeared from the window, also in a heap of trouble. I felt awful, and I knew one day I'd have to take one for the team to make it up to her. I followed Daniel to the porch, where he sat his helmet on the porch swing.

"Goodbye, old friend," he said, patting it before opening the door to let me in.

"Why are you telling your helmet goodbye?" I asked.

"It's been good to me, Peaches, but when your Dad's through with me, I probably won't be able to walk, let alone ride a bike again," he said.

"Don't be silly, Daniel. He's an ER doctor, not a mob boss," I said, letting the screen door slam behind us. Rose was already on the sofa, waiting for the two of us to discover our punishments. I sat beside her, and Daniel took the seat on the other side of me. He pressed himself against the arm of the sofa, doing his best to get as far away from me as possible while my father stared him down.

"Explain," Dad ordered.

I swallowed hard. I didn't fear my father, but I did hate the idea of disappointing him. He was as laid back as anyone could be, and he trusted his daughters to do the right thing. When we didn't, he had a way of making us feel worse about it by simply *being* disappointed.

"We were watching television and accidentally fell asleep on the couch," I said.

"Yeah? I've used that excuse myself a few times. What were you watching?" he asked Daniel, trying to poke holes in our story.

"Monty Python, sir," he said. "Flying Circus on DVD. My grandfather got them for me a long time ago. They're one of my favorites and... um... So yeah, that's what we were watching."

My father seemed slightly surprised by this and questioned him further. "Which episode?"

"Season one. I think Peach—I mean, Hazel, fell asleep on episode four. I don't remember episode five, so I'd say I fell asleep right after learning how to defend against people with fresh fruit," he responded, giving a much more detailed answer than I would have, but I assumed he was nervous.

"Good gosh," Rose whispered under her breath. "He's gonna get us both grounded for life."

"Too bad. I quite like episode five. Confuse a cat is... Wait, what am I saying? I'm trying to interrogate you. Stop telling me about Monty Python!" Dad shook his head and turned his focus to me. "Why were you climbing the ladder instead of owning your mistake and coming through the front door?"

I wanted to scream *Rose told me to,* but that was hardly fair to my sister, who did her best to keep me out of trouble. "I'm not sure. I guess I didn't want to get into trouble."

"Well, now look at you. You almost got hurt, and now you're in bigger trouble than you would've been if you'd only told the truth. Accidents happen, Hazel. I'd like to think your mother and I are cool, understanding parents who don't overreact to mistakes. Next time, just tell me the truth."

"Yes, sir," I said, then he turned his attention to Rose.

"And you, young lady, don't ever lie to us again. Did you know where she was when you told us she went to bed?" he asked.

"No, sir," Rose responded, hanging her head.

"What if something had happened to her, Rose? We wouldn't have known until morning, maybe too late." He glanced at all of us, then asked, "So, what's the moral of the story here?" When no one answered, Dad said, "I'm waiting for a brilliant response from someone."

Daniel cleared his throat. "Just be honest," he said.

"Yes, Daniel. Thank you." Dad sat on the ottoman across from us with his elbows on his knees. He chewed the inside of his mouth for a few minutes while he pondered our punishment. He decided to leave the ball in our court, giving us a chance to plead our case. "Now, what do I do? What do the three of you think I should do here?"

Daniel looked at me, then back to my father. "M-me, too?" he asked.

"Yeah, you too. Where are your parents right now?" Dad asked.

"Dad, no idea. Mom is with my sister in Florida for a doctor's appointment," he admitted.

"Well, then I guess that makes me your warden until she returns, doesn't it?" Dad asked, sitting up straighter.

"But I'm eighteen, and I can—" I covered Daniel's mouth with my hand, deciding to save him the trouble of digging his own grave.

"She's coming back tomorrow afternoon, Dad," I informed him.

"Perfect, until then... uh..." Dad stammered, looking a little confused. "Until then, I have no idea."

"I'm not sure, but I think this is the part where you ground Hazel and Rose and let the poor guy who saved Hazel's life off with a warning," Daniel said after he pried my hands off his face.

"Is that so?" my father chuckled. "And what kind of punishment do you propose, Daniel?" My father was enjoying every moment of his interaction with my quirky friend. I, on the other hand, feared Daniel would say something insane, and my father would agree to it, like sentencing me to life with no ice cream.

Daniel smirked, realizing it was all one big joke to my father at that point—after all, he'd accomplished what he set out to do. Rose and I felt awful for disappointing him, and we would both be on our best behavior for at least... oh, maybe a week or so.

"Well, sir, it should be painful, you know? Really hit them where it hurts, like, say, only letting Hazel hang out with me for the next two weeks," Daniel said.

"How is that a punishment?" my father asked.

"Have you spent more than five minutes with him? It's torture!" Rose squawked.

Daniel threw a pillow over me and nailed Rose in the head, making my father laugh. Rose dove over my lap and tackled Daniel to the ground in an act of violence I'd never seen my sister display before. She wailed at my friend with both fists, pummeling his arm and shoulders while he laughed at her maniacally.

"Okay, okay, enough," Dad said, still laughing. "In all seriousness, in the future, please call your mother or me. Tell the truth, and it'll be a lot easier on you, okay?"

"Wait... does that mean we're not grounded?" I asked.

"This time, but if it happens again, you don't want to know what I'll do." He turned his attention to Daniel. "Go get your bike and put it in the garage. No way I'm letting you ride that thing across town at one in the morning."

"Sir?" Daniel asked.

"Park it, and Hazel will show you the guest room. Or would you rather I call your mother?" Dad asked.

"Nope, I'm good." Daniel was off the sofa and out the front door to get his bike before my father had a chance to take another breath.

Rose rolled her eyes, then looked at me. "Do me a favor. Next time, set the alarm on your phone, *Peaches.*"

"Don't call her Peaches!" Daniel yelled from the porch, probably waking our neighbors.

Rose sighed and rolled her eyes again. "Why, Hazel?"

"Why what?" I asked.

"Why, out of all the boys in the world, did you go and fall for the one that annoys me the most?" she teased, then left the room before I had the chance to deny her claim. I heard the rumble of the bike in the garage, and it hit me. *Daniel was spending the night at my house.* It made my stomach flutter, and my heart did a flippy floppy dance. Rose was right. I didn't just like Daniel; I fell for him hook, line, and sinker. I could deny it or try to hide it all I wanted, but it was true.

He came through the kitchen door, the one that led to the garage, and walked up to me.

"Your Dad's pretty cool for a Dad, not that I have much to compare him to," he said.

"Yeah. He's... he's great," I said. "I'll show you the room."

We had about five hours before we had to get up for school, and I seriously doubted I would sleep for a single minute. I'd be too busy wondering what Daniel was thinking about in the room next door to mine.

Rose's door was already closed, probably fast asleep since she didn't have a confusing boy in her life. Tee was simple, honest, and straightforward. I, on the other hand, was too scared to even admit my feelings to myself, let alone to Daniel.

Daniel settled on the bed and stared at the ceiling. "See you soon, Peaches," he said, glancing at me.

"Yeah," I said, turning out the light. "Soon."

I started to shut the door, but he called my name. "Peaches?"

"Yeah?"

"Can you come here a minute?" he asked, sitting up in the bed. I hesitated, figuring I was already on thin ice with my parents, and getting caught in the room with him after I'd been ordered to go to bed would probably be really bad. "Just a minute, I promise."

I walked over to the bed in the dark, wondering why I didn't turn the light on first, then answered my own question immediately when I realized he couldn't see my face in the dimly lit room. "Yes?" I asked.

"Can I ask you a really random question?"

"All of your questions are really random, so what's one more?" I teased.

"Very funny, Peaches. Seriously, it's not gonna make sense, but I need to know. Last year, the secret Valentine thing, did you get anything?" he asked.

"Sure, everyone did," I responded. He was right, it was a very random question.

"Who was it from?" he asked.

"It was secret, remember?"

"But you must have some idea of who sent it, right?"

"It was a dozen fuchsia-colored peonies. There are only two people in the school who know that's my absolute favorite flower, my sister and Ronin. It wasn't Rose, so I assumed it was Ronin. Why do you ask?"

"Is that why you started dating him?"

"No, not really. I mean, we started talking more after that, and eventually, we started dating, but not for a couple of months. What brought all this up, Daniel?" It was all out of place and a bizarre conversation to be having at one in the morning.

"Just wondering. Night, Peaches," he said, then slid down in the bed and kicked his shoes off. He reached for the blankets while I stood there, staring at him in the darkness.

When I could think of nothing to say, I turned around to head to my own room. "Peaches?"

"Yes, Daniel?"

"I didn't get a good night, hug," he whined.

"I'm sorry, I didn't know that was a thing," I whispered, sure my parents would come and murder us both.

"It's not, so I'm making it a thing now." He sat back up, and I met him at the bed, wrapping my arms around his neck. He slid his around my waist and pulled me tightly against him. "I'm happy we're friends. You know that, right?"

He was acting so strange—more than the usual amount of Daniel strange. I wanted to question him, but I knew I wouldn't get any answers, nothing more than, *oh, look at the time*—his usual response. So, I admitted I would never really fully understand Daniel and nodded.

"I do, and I'm glad we're friends, too," I said. He looked up at me, and in the moonlight, I could make out how dark his eyes were—a deep, almost forest green highlighted with the usual honey-gold. "We should get some sleep."

He released me quickly, like a scalded cat. "Night again, Peaches."

"Goodnight, Daniel."

I made it all the way to the door this time and closed it behind me before he could do anything else that would make me want to stay in there talking to him all night. Once in the comfort of my own bed, I fell asleep much faster than I thought I would, which would prove to be a blessing when morning rolled around.

Thirteen

"Tell your best friend to quit hogging the cereal, Peaches!" Rose shouted over the commotion in the kitchen. Four teenagers, two adults, and one small kitchen made for a rough start to the day.

"Stop calling her Peaches, and I'll give you the box!" Daniel shouted at Rose while Dizzy tried, and failed, to reach the box he held over their heads.

"Kids, can you not?" my mother asked, rubbing her forehead with the back of her hand.

"Gimmie it, giant, tree-sized boy!" Rose yelled again.

"Tree-sized boy? Is that the best you can come up with micro human?" Daniel teased, lowering the box a fraction of an inch but still just out of reach. Rose and Dizzy both jumped to reach but were no match for the towering boy.

I sighed. "Daniel, would you please?"

He smirked at the two and handed them the box without question.

"Really? You're not scoring a lot of brownie points with the sister, doofus," Rose snapped, but I saw her bite back a smile when she turned away.

"You love it, you just don't know it yet. You'll get used to it," he said, handing me a bowl of cereal. I was so sick of eating cereal for breakfast, but anything else required work, and work required getting out of bed long before I felt like it. "I gotta bolt anyway."

"What? Why?" I asked.

"I'd kinda like to shower and wear different clothes today, Peaches," Daniel said.

"You'll be late for school. I'm sure we can find you something to wear today," Mom said, more a command than an offer. Luckily, Daniel picked up on her tone as well, and responded with a nod and, "Yes ma'am."

She wandered off in search of something my father wouldn't miss while the rest of us ate in silence. Noting but clanking spoons and crunching for five minutes, then the kitchen erupted again. The doorbell rang, and Rose yelled, "Come in!"

Tee poked his head in, "Hey, it's raining."

"Wow, observant," Daniel said. "Do you have any other superpowers we should know about?"

Rose smacked Daniel's arm hard. "Shut up, you tree-sized doofus." I rolled my eyes as the two went back to irritating one another relentlessly. Dizzy joined in the effort, but Daniel took them both on, trading jabs and smart remarks like any proper big brother would.

"Hey, Tee, how's it going?" I asked.

He shuffled around a little, then said, "Good, just getting ready for playoffs now. Is it always like this first thing in the morning?" He pointed to the three idiots arguing over who was the smartest—little did they know.

"Today is a first, but I have a feeling it will only get worse from here," I said, laughing at them. Tee chuckled and shook his head. It made me happy to know he wasn't my friend solely to date my sister and that he genuinely cared about my feelings through the whole break-up with Ronin and losing my position on the team.

"So, listen, I wanted to tell you I was talking with Ronin last night, and I don't think he'll be bothering you anymore," Tee said.

"You mean attacking me for no reason? How wonderful. How did you manage that?" I asked.

"Let's just say a few points were made very clear, and he knows he's been way out of line. I think right now all he wants is to know you're happy, and one day you might forgive him for being stupid," he said.

He was acting a little shifty, like someone who knew more than they were letting on but would die before revealing their secrets. "Points were made clear?" I asked.

"It was brought to his attention that he hurt you deeply, and his actions were continuing that pain for no reason. You're obviously happy with Daniel, so he's gonna back off and move on. Maybe one day you can be friends again, but he knows that won't be for a very long time."

Tee refused to admit that he was the one who'd set Ronin straight, though I couldn't think of anyone else who'd get through to him so easily. It had to be him. "Thanks, Tee."

"Sure," he said, then got Rose's attention. "Rose, we should go since it's raining. I don't want to rush." I got the feeling he wanted to change topics, and getting his new girlfriend's attention would do that. Rose gave Daniel one last demonic glare, then followed Tee out the door. My Dad threw a shirt at Daniel, then dragged my mother out the door, leaving Dizzy, Daniel, and me to our own devices.

"Any chance I can catch a ride with you guys? I'm not interested in crashing my bike in this torrential downpour," Daniel said, rolling up the sleeves of my father's shirt repeatedly. My father was an inch or so shorter than Daniel, but his arms must have been longer because the sleeves of the shirt kept falling over his hands.

"I have my car, so he's all yours, Peaches," Dizzy said, then practically ran out the door before Daniel could make her pay for stealing his nickname for me again. He shouted at her, but she slammed the door in his face. He looked back at me with a frustrated sigh.

"Why is everyone trying to steal Peaches from me?" he asked.

"Oh, stop. No one is going to steal me from you, Daniel," I said, slipping the straps of my bag over my shoulders. He grinned, the one I loved.

"I meant the nickname, but it's nice to know you're all mine," he said. I felt my cheeks warm. "We better go, or we'll be late."

We made a mad dash to my car because I forgot my umbrella and didn't feel like disarming the home alarm and resetting it just to go in for an umbrella. It turned out okay, though. I quite enjoyed him picking me up and running to the car with me. It was a good thing he wasn't as clumsy as me, or it would have been a painful run to the car. Once inside, he shook his head like a dog, splattering water all over the inside of my car.

"Daniel!"

"What? It's water, Peaches. It'll dry," he said.

"It'll stain the upholstery," I whined.

"Maybe you don't pay attention in chemistry class, but water is a clear liquid often used in cleaning things that are dirty," he stared at me, waiting for me to bounce back with some sass of my own, but I wasn't feeling it. "No banter today?" he asked.

"Maybe later. I'm tired from our late-night antics," I said.

"Our late-night antics, you say? Pray, tell, what antics do you speak of? The ones where you threw your shoe at me and left this bruise?" He brushed the hair from his forehead to show me my handy work. A yellowish bruise spread across part of it.

"Oops, sorry," I said, pulling onto the main road from our neighborhood.

"Or maybe the whole incident where your Dad did that super weird non-grounding thing, then let me spend the night in the same house as his two teenage daughters?"

"Meh, he'd have killed you if you'd tried anything," I said.

"Or the fact that you snore really loudly and—"

"I do not!" I yelled. "That was Rose, I'll have you know! And if this is your attempt at getting me to banter with you, then... you got me." I sighed and turned onto the street our school was on.

"Oh, before I forget, this weekend is a lunar eclipse, and I was wondering if your super-cool, non-weird parents would let you watch it on the beach with me?" he asked. "You'd be out past curfew."

"I can ask, but probably," I said, parking the car as close to the front as possible but not nearly close enough to stay dry. "We're gonna get soaked. I'm glad I keep a change of clothes in my locker."

"You keep a change of clothes in your locker? Do you often require changing?" he teased.

"Yes, Daniel. I'm like a doll. I require at least four outfit changes a day, a dream house, and a pink car." I joked, giving in and giving him the snarky side of me he wanted. I grabbed my things, pushed the door open, slammed it closed, and ran as fast as I could toward the front door. If I was lucky, I'd only get moderately soaked.

Daniel caught up to me and grabbed my hand, stopping me short. "Daniel! It's pouring!"

"I know, and it's not an opportunity I want to miss." He pulled me close and wrapped his arms around my waist, pulling me up to meet his lips. He ignored the rain and kissed me until I couldn't breathe, then let me slide to the ground, barely touching it with my toes. I struggled to regain my composure and glanced around to make sure no teachers saw.

"Sorry," he said. "I couldn't help myself. I wanted to get in one more good jab."

I barely registered the rain pelting my face as I looked up at him. "Huh?"

He nodded toward the front of the school, where Ronin stood with Tee. His gaze was sorrowful but not angry like it used to be. My heart sank, heavy in my chest. I didn't care what Ronin thought, I only cared that the kiss was all for show—again.

"You okay, Peaches?" Daniel asked.

"Yeah, fine. That was... I don't think we really need to rub it in anymore, you know? I'm over him, so..." I didn't know what else to say. I loved kissing Daniel, but with every passing day, I knew the more we pretended to be together, the harder it would be to say goodbye. And we would have to say goodbye at some point because he had plans, and I only had vague ideas of what I wanted with my life.

"Hey," he said, lifting my chin. "I didn't mean to make this awkward. Let's go, so you have time to change," he said. Once under cover of the awning, he hugged me. "I'll let you know about Becca's appointment when I know something. See you at lunch, Peaches."

I waved at him as he retreated, and the warning bell rang. So much for changing before class. I made my way quickly to my first class and shuffled in, soaking wet. Sara was already in her seat, and because she's an awful person, she covered her nose and said, "Ew, does anyone else smell wet dog?"

A few people chuckled, but most people ignored her. I sat close to the back, under the air vent, with the hope it would dry me a little faster. The class dragged along, probably because my jeans were wet and annoying, so time decided to make me suffer as long as possible. Finally, the bell rang, and I bolted out, desperate to get to my locker to change before the second period.

That was the plan, but Sara happened. It seemed Sara or Ronin were always in my way when I had things to do. "Stop right there!" she shouted at me.

"Excuse me?"

"You heard me. We need to talk," Sara said, her hair an even brighter shade of blonde than before. If she kept on, it would either go white or fall out by prom.

"I don't have anything to say to you, Sara. You said your piece with the twenty-seven text messages you sent, but you should know it was a waste of your time. I don't want Ronin," I said, turning to walk away.

"You say that like he was an option. Well, he wasn't. He's mine, and he's happy now," she said.

"You know, you keep saying that, but he keeps telling me he doesn't like you. I think you're trying awfully hard to prove a point that doesn't exist, Sara." I said, still walking to my locker. I didn't have time for her—enough was enough already.

She caught up to me and grabbed my bag, jerking me back. "Sara, let go of me. Get over yourself already and leave me alone." I started to walk again, but she stopped me again.

"I'm not done talking to you. I'm telling you one last time, stay away from him, or else," Sara snapped.

I stared into her eyes, such a change from a few weeks ago when I thought we were friends. "You know what, Sara? I think all that bleach you're using has gone to your brain."

She snickered. "At least I'm not dating a loser. Seriously, where did you find that guy?"

I resisted the urge to punch her in the face, choosing instead to be the bigger person. Turns out, I had more people in my corner than I realized. A random girl I had never spoken to in my life, passed us in the hall and said, "She got him from Hot Guys R Us, right down the street from You're a Horrible Person."

"Excuse me?" Sara spat, "Who do you think you are?"

"Just a random spectator; don't mind me," she said, the bright green stripe in her hair making her look like a rock star paired with her faded band t-shirt. The girl started to walk away but turned back and said, "By the way, you've got something on your butt."

Sara turned and twisted around to see what it could be. When she found nothing, she glared at her. "There's nothing there."

The girl licked her finger and wiped a lipstick smudge from Sara's face. "Sorry, I meant your face. It's so hard to tell the difference." With that, my new idol walked down the hall and into her classroom. I shrugged at Sara and left her standing there, huffing and puffing.

Unfortunately, there was no time to change after my pleasant interaction with Sara. I'd have to suffer through another class with wet clothes, but I did make a mental note to figure out who the fantastic person was who intervened on my behalf. I chuckled, thinking of her, but it was not enough to take my mind off my damp jeans. I wished they'd hurry and dry because every time I thought about them, I thought about rain, and thinking about the rain made me think of Daniel and that amazing kiss.

The second before I stepped into class, my phone vibrated in my pocket. I pulled it out and swiped to read the messages Daniel sent me.

Daniel

> *Bad news. Becca's appointment did not go well.*
> *Her condition is too advanced for the trial. Not*
> *feeling school today. Going home.*

My heart sank again, feeling awful for Becca. She seemed like a lovely person, and I had prayed so hard that the treatment would be an option for her. Surely, other options could be explored. I responded to his text, debating whether I even wanted to go to class. He had to be miserable, and I didn't want him to be so sad and stuck alone.

> *Now what? What else is there to try?*

I slipped away from the door, going unnoticed by the teacher. Maybe I could go to the nurse's office and pretend I was sick? My stomach wasn't all that happy after getting Daniel's messages, so I could probably pull it off.

> *This was the last option. There's nothing left to*
> *try. Becca will be totally blind by her seventeenth*
> *birthday. Meet me after school, and tell me all the*
> *details about Sara's takedown.*

I'd all but forgotten about the cheer regulations with the rain kiss and my confrontation with the devil herself. There was no way I was doing it without him. It was thanks to him I even had a chance of getting my spot back.

> *It can wait until tomorrow. I'll call you soon.*

I stuffed my phone in my pocket and called my Dad, begging him to get me an early dismissal. "Dad, I promise it's for a good reason. I'll come to the hospital and explain," I said.

"Fine, be here in twenty minutes, Hazel. I mean it, no running off and thinking I'll just let it go again, got me?"

"Yes, sir," I said, heading toward the door. There were specialists at the hospital, maybe they could help Becca? I wanted to try because I felt useless. Daniel was upset, and I couldn't do anything to change it, which made me feel like the world's worst best friend.

I hoped I didn't run any red lights on the way to the hospital because I didn't recall seeing any lights at all. I parked outside the ER and hurried through the double doors. "Hey, Georgia, can I see my father?" I asked the receptionist, who'd known me since the day Rose and I were born.

"Sure, honey. Go on back." She buzzed me into the back, and I found him typing notes into a computer in the nurse's station, grumbling at the screen when it didn't display what he wanted. His lips pursed and forehead narrowed, I wasn't sure it was the best time to interrupt him, but I had no choice.

"Daddy?" I caught his attention, but he only held up a finger until he was finished typing. When he was done, he dropped his stethoscope on the desk and walked around the island to meet me. He hugged me tightly and motioned toward the lounge area.

Once inside, he asked, "What's this about, honey? You seem frazzled. Are you feeling okay?"

"What can you do to help someone with Stargardt disease?" I asked, getting right to the point.

"Stargardt?" he asked. "Who has that?"

"Daniel's sister. She's in Florida right now, at the Mayo Clinic. I guess there was some experimental something or other, but they said her condition was too advanced. I'm not sure what that means, but she already can't see anything clearly," I said.

"Oh, honey, I'm so sorry. It means there won't be anything that can be done to save her vision. I'm afraid Daniel's sister's vision will be severely impaired unless new treatments are developed," he said, sitting on the sofa beside me.

"There has to be something? Anything?" I begged.

"No, Hazel, I'm afraid there's not. Perhaps one day, a treatment will be discovered, but right now, there just isn't one that can help someone with a case that advanced. The best thing you can do is help her amplify her other senses. Studies that show people who lose vision eventually have increased auditory functions, and even tactile senses and taste can be improved."

"What good is that when you can't see, Dad? What will she do now?" I scoffed.

"A lot of good, Hazel. Just because she lost her sight doesn't mean she's doomed to fail in life, honey. There are a lot of blind people who use their other senses, and in many ways, they are better at their craft than those with all five senses. I'll remind you, some of my favorite musicians were blind," he teased, reminding me of the days he used to make Rose and me listen to blues on the car ride home from school.

"What can I do to help her with that?" I asked.

"Remind her that she's still a whole person and support her through the depression that's bound to come," he said, but I had no idea how to do that. How does one support someone whose depression stems from something I could never really understand? What could I do to show her I was in her corner? My father's mention of blind musicians got me thinking.

"Daddy? Can I use my emergency credit card for something?" I asked.

"Define something."

"A gift for Becca, something that can help her feel in control of her future. Something to show her she can still do things," I said.

He thought for a moment. "Okay, but you have to pay us back by the end of summer."

"Deal. Can I also stay out for the rest of the day? I promise I won't ask again." He gave me a warning look.

"You're pushing the envelope here, but since it's for a good cause, I'll allow it just this once. You can't go around breaking curfew and skipping school, especially in your senior year. You've followed the rules all your life, kiddo. I don't know how to ground disobedient kids," he said, chuckling. He stood and opened the lounge door, so he could get back to work.

"Hazel?" he said as I passed.

"Yeah, Dad?"

"I'm proud of you, honey. I'm proud of the person you are. Don't ever change."

He couldn't have known what his words meant to me, and he couldn't have known just how much I needed to hear them from someone who'd known me all my life.

I raced to my car and drove to the music store downtown. I had no idea how much money I was about to drop on someone I hardly knew, but I felt compelled to do it anyway. The door dinged—why? Why did doors always ding? Especially when the ding did nothing to gain the attention of the extremely bored-looking college-aged guy behind the desk.

"Hello? Can you help me, please?" I asked as I smacked the bell on the counter. So many bells, but none seemed to catch his attention. "Hello!" I waved my hands around until he finally saw me from the corner of his eye.

"Oh, sorry. Didn't hear you come in." He pulled a set of earbuds from his ears and closed the magazine he was looking through. "What can I do for you?"

"I'm looking for an instrument for a friend. She's, well, she's going blind and... I don't know what I'm doing, really. I just want to help her," I said, hoping somehow he would understand what I was trying to do.

He stared at me for a moment, but not as if I were a strange person interrupting his day of doing nothing, but instead contemplating my rambling. "I'd go with a violin, I think. The sound is close to the ear, and she'll enjoy it more. It will help her intensify her auditory range, which is what I assume your goal is?"

"Exactly!" I shouted, glad he made sense of my word jumble.

"Happens more than you'd think. I'd go with this one." He handed me a slim violin that was pretty but not overly ornate. "It's not expensive, and it's a good beginner style. Pair that with this, and you've got a good start for a blind student." He handed me a book of CDs titled *Learning to Play by Ear: A Beginner's Tool*.

"This was far less painful than I anticipated. Thank you so much," I said.

"Sure, and when she's ready, we have classes every Friday night for both sighted and non-sighted learners," he added. "Let me get this charged up, and I'll box it for you."

I left the store with a brand-new violin and high hopes for Becca. I drove much more carefully to Daniel's house and realized he'd walked all the way there from school since his bike was still at my home. He'd probably be tired in addition to upset, but I hoped I could cheer him up, if only a little. I rang the doorbell and waited with my surprise in hand. It had stopped raining, and the sun was trying hard to peek through the clouds.

The door opened, and Daniel smiled. "Peaches! What are you doing here?" He pulled me into the house in a bear hug, almost making me drop the box.

"Don't worry. I got permission from my Dad to skip. I'm all yours until you feel like kicking me out," I said, settling on the sofa he'd dropped me onto.

"What's that?" he asked, pointing to the box.

"A gift for your sister! I talked to my Dad. He said the best thing we can do is help Becca learn to amplify her other senses, so I thought, why not learn to play an instrument? Look, there are CDs and Braille books and everything, so she can learn something new to help her cope with losing her vision. The guy at the store said there are classes every Friday for beginners, even for those who are visually impaired. If she is interested, I got the card from—"

"Whoa, Peaches, take a breath," he said, laughing.

I was too busy selling the idea to breathe, so I took a deep inhale and glanced back at the box. Daniel opened it and peered at his sister's new violin. He grazed his fingers over the shiny wood and looked up at me. "You did all this for my sister? You barely know her."

"Well, yeah," I said, then grew concerned. "Oh, no. Is it too much? Did I go overboard again? I'm sorry if I overstepped or went too far."

He shook his head, his hazel eyes watery. So much so, I thought he might be holding back tears. He blinked, confirming my suspicions as fat tears slipped over his cheeks.

He sighed and pulled me into another hug. "No, Peaches. It's just the right amount of much."

Fourteen

B ecca's gift went over even better than I'd expected. Once
she and her mother arrived home, she stormed to her
room and slammed the door. I met Ms. Starnes for the first time
when Daniel shoved me in her face and announced that I was
the most amazing person in the world. She sighed, tired and
disappointed, but she did her best to make me feel welcome
even though her son was wired for sound and bouncing off the
walls. She had no idea why until he showed her what I had
gotten for her daughter.

Ms. Starnes' mood was instantly improved, and she agreed
with Daniel that I was, in fact, the most amazing person in the
world. By the time I left to head home for dinner, Becca had
cried twice, laughed until she snorted four times, and thanked
me half a million times. She began immediately, in dire need of
something to distract her from the pain of knowing she would
never clearly again. I imagined it was more challenging to lose
your vision than to have never had it at all, but I suppose, in the
end, it's all the same—gone is gone—and in Becca's words, I'd
given her a chance to see through music.

If I'd known how awful it would sound, I would have left before she picked up the bow. But I believed she would learn, and I convinced Daniel I was right. His delight with my gift did a total one-eighty after two solid hours of listening to Becca screeching away on her new violin. I do believe he would have wrung my neck if his mother were not present, but every time he heard her laugh at her mistake, his heart warmed a little, and he eased up on the death glares sent my way. When his mother told him she planned to take Becca to visit their grandparents in the morning, his jovial mood returned.

He rode back to my house with me to retrieve his bike, reminding me of my promise to let him have a front-row seat to Sara's devastation, which brought me to the moment I'd been waiting for.

The next day, I scheduled a meeting with the cheer coach at lunch, during which she agreed with my assessment of the regulation. She also agreed we would discuss it with the team after school, just before practice.

Sara's platinum blonde hair appeared before she did, the shocking, unnatural color demanding attention. She saw me seated beside Daniel and didn't bother to hide her disgust. "What are you doing here?"

"I invited her. Girls, let's have a seat. We have a few things to discuss before practice," Coach said.

They all gathered, taking seats on the bleachers. They looked downright miserable, and I would soon find out why. The coach stood in front with her clipboard and a copy of the handbook. "It has been brought to my attention that competition regulation states that no qualified team may change their line-up less than sixty days before regionals, except for injury. Miss Simmons appears healthy enough, so I'm assuming there is some other reason you all voted to replace her? Or are you just silly enough to throw away your chance at a bid to nationals over a boy?"

"I'm sorry, we have no idea what you're talking about. Hazel resigned," Sara said. The other girls kept quiet, though, from the looks on their faces, this was all news to them.

Coach sighed and dropped her clipboard to the ground. Her hands went to her face, and she let out a frustrated groan. When she removed her hands, she said, "I'm not sure why students think teachers have no idea what goes on around here, but let me enlighten you. We know all about the drama surrounding Ronin McKinsey, Sara. It's hard to miss a four-layer chocolate cake smashed on the floor."

She crossed her arms and continued her speech. "I highly doubt Miss Simmons resigned her position after working so hard to get us to regionals, so don't insult my intelligence with weak excuses. I'm going to make this very simple. You have a choice, continue on with Sara as your captain and give up your chance to win a national title, or reinstate Hazel effective immediately. All those in favor of reinstatement, please raise your hand."

Every hand but Sara's shot up, and Erin raised both.

"Excuse me, Coach?" Erin asked.

"Yes, Erin?"

"I think I can speak for everyone when I request a second vote, one which leads to Sara's dismissal from the team," she said.

"Dismissal?" Coach asked.

"Yes, please," Miriam added. "She's a gigantic... thing I can't say without getting detention, but she knows what she is."

"You can't vote to kick me off the team. I worked just as hard as Hazel did!" Sara screeched. "Just because she found a loophole doesn't make her a better captain than me!"

"You're right. You're absolutely right," Ashley said. "But I'm pretty sure her choreography, her patience, and her ability to not be a raging... that word Miriam can't say do qualify her as a better captain."

"It doesn't matter, you still can't kick me off the team unless the captain approves, and Hazel knows better than to try that," Sara spat.

"Hazel isn't the only one who can approve a dismissal," Daniel said, standing from his seat and stepping down the bleachers. "May I?" he asked Coach, pointing to the handbook. She nodded, and he flipped through the pages.

"It says here that if the captain is unable to be reached, the team coach has the final say," Daniel said, handing the book over. "I believe that's you, madam." He bowed and walked back to the bleachers, leaning against the guard rail—then he covered my mouth so I could not speak when Coach addressed me.

"Interesting, it seems I cannot reach Hazel." Coach said. "Sara, don't let the door hit you on the way out."

"What?" Sara screamed, but it was futile. Everyone was already walking away, heading outdoors to practice.

Coach patted my shoulder as I passed, heading to the locker room to change. "Glad you're back, Simmons. I shouldn't say this, but Sara's a piece of work, and I'm glad she's gone."

I smiled, happy to be back where I belonged. Daniel ran up and hugged me from behind, then picked me up and spun me around. "I'm so happy for you!" His excitement was interrupted by Erin, who approached sheepishly.

"Hi, Hazel." She shifted around a few times, then said, "I know we were all wrong, the way we handled everything, I mean. Sara had us all believing a load of things that just weren't true, and I'm truly sorry. If it's any consolation, it's been misery without you."

"Thanks, Erin. I'm sorry it was so bad." I glanced at Daniel, and I knew then and there that I had grown so much in the short time I'd known him. That gave me the strength to be honest. "Even so, this is a working relationship. I'll help you win regionals, maybe nationals if we're lucky, but that's it. We can't be friends again."

Her face drooped, but she accepted what she already knew would happen. "I understand, and I'm still glad you're back. At least now we have a chance." She jogged off, leaving me alone with Daniel again.

"Look at my Peaches using that backbone." He nudged my shoulder. "I'm proud of you, you know that? A week ago, you would have caved and been besties with the witches again."

"I wouldn't call them witches, maybe just—"

"Stupid?" he offered.

I chuckled. "Okay, yeah, stupid for sure, but not witches."

"Whatever, I'm still really proud of you," he said. "And so happy you got back something you deserve. Now, go choreograph some super awesome cheer and call me later."

"Your mom and Becca head out this morning?" I asked, remembering they planned to visit his grandparents in Virginia.

"Yep, and she took that violin with her, thank goodness," he joked.

I shook my head and jogged to the locker room, so ready to put the team through the wringer during practice. Two hours later, they begged for mercy, but it wasn't my fault they couldn't keep up. I had so many ideas for the regional choreography that I couldn't contain my excitement. Eventually, Coach had to step in and remind me that injuries happened when people were tired. I dismissed practice and headed to the locker room to change.

Sometimes, when you least expect it, someone does something so outrageous you can hardly believe it happened. But it does. And when it does, you have to figure out how to fix the mess. That's what I had to do after Sara, in a fit of rage, snuck into the showers and literally cut my hair off. The girls didn't see her, they were all busy showering or packing their bags. She snuck in, grabbed my long hair, and in one swipe, she'd cut nearly all of it to shoulder length. My blood-curdling scream gained Coach's attention and earned Sara a five-day suspension. The girls tried to talk me into pressing assault charges against Sara, but it wouldn't bring my hair back.

Ashley trimmed it as best she could, but I'd have to get it cut soon. There were worse things Sara could have done, like stabbing me to death with the scissors, but it was still upsetting. After the events of the day, followed by my impromptu style change, I decided a little one-on-one time with my twin was sorely needed.

She had a great new boyfriend, and I hardly heard anything about it. We needed some bonding time, and I needed her to fix the mess Sara made. I sent Daniel a text message informing him of my change of plans. He wasn't all that happy about my run-in, but he let it go after a little begging.

Rose did an excellent job, but my hair ended up barely grazing my shoulders by the time she finished. After much assurance that I looked beautiful and spilling her guts about her relationship with Tee, we parted ways for bed. I, however, could not sleep a wink. I had too much going on in my head to sleep—new routine ideas, pent-up anger with Sara, ideas for prom—so much stuff that I needed to talk about.

After an hour of tossing, I got up and got dressed, snuck downstairs, and made it outside without getting caught. I have no idea what possessed me to sneak out of my house, but I did,

and that would prove to be a huge mistake. I had lost my mind
along with my hair, but all I could think about was seeing Daniel,
thanking him for what he'd done for me, and telling him all about
my ideas. I finally felt like me again, thanks to his help.

I drove to Daniel's house, not bothering to text him first. I
parked along the street, then ran up the front stairs. With his
mother and sister out of town again, he was probably still awake
binge-watching television shows he didn't want to admit he
watched. I knocked on the door several times, and he finally
opened it.

"Peaches, what's wrong?" His sleepy voice was laced with
concern as he pulled me into his house by my arm. His even
sleepier eyes scanned me, making sure nothing was physically
wrong with me. I didn't anticipate that he would be asleep.

"Nothing's wrong. I just had a bunch of stuff I wanted to talk
about, like prom and a new cheer routine. I had this cool idea,
and I wanted to see what you thought," I said breathlessly, only
then noticing that I was rambling.

His eyebrows arched. "And you thought two in the morning
was the appropriate time to relay all of this information to
me? Couldn't have waited until morning, like, I don't know, at
school?"

I looked at the clock on his wall, and my jaw dropped. "Oh my
gosh, it's two a.m.? I had no idea it was so late. I'm sorry, Daniel."
He was right. What was I doing out so late on a school night?
Why couldn't I sleep until I spoke to him? Saw him?

"No worries, Peaches. Okay, then, morning it is," he said, then
ushered me toward the door yawning.

"Wait, but you're already awake, so maybe I could just tell
you..."

He stopped short. "Seriously, Peaches? Are you kidding? I
thought something was seriously wrong when I saw you standing

here at two in the morning. It scared the snot out of me, but now that I know it's just a cheer thing... can't it wait?"

His voice was short and irritated, just like Ronan's had been the day of the balloon fiasco. It took me by surprise, especially since it was so out of character for him. His face was tired, but there was also the annoyance and irritation I'd seen on Ronin's face the day he broke up with me. This was it, the moment Daniel finally saw me the same way Ronin did.

"Forget it." I snapped and walked out the door, slamming it behind me. He opened it again, following me down the front stairs to the walkway.

"Peaches!" he yelled, then chased me down the walkway to the sidewalk, catching me by the arm. "Are you kidding me right now? What is wrong with you?"

I jerked my arm away, knowing full well he didn't deserve my anger, but it was so pent-up inside I couldn't control it. I was so tired of being viewed as an over-the-top nutcase I didn't bother to consider just how out of line I was by showing up unannounced at two in the morning. I continued my march to my car, frustrated with myself, with Ronin and Sara, with everything.

"I'm not him, you know," Daniel said behind me, his voice strained.

I stopped at the edge of the sidewalk, one step away from my car. "What?" I asked.

He gently pulled on my shoulder, turning me around to face him. "I'm not him. I'm not Ronin, Peaches."

"I know you're not, Daniel," I said, an edge to my voice.

"I don't think you do. I can see it in the way you look at me. It's like you're waiting for the other shoe to drop for me to tell you you've done something wrong. I'm not him," he said again.

"And I'm not ever going to *be* him. I won't leave you just because you do something annoying."

"They why are you acting like him right now?" I asked. I felt my chest tighten. Daniel didn't deserve to be yelled at, especially not at his own home in the middle of the night.

"I'm not, Peaches. You are an amazing person, you know that. You don't need me to tell you that, but I will anyway because I want to. Everything you do is incredible, but that's not the problem. The problem is—" I jerked my car door open, not caring to hear any more complaints about me and my personality issues. He stopped me again, determined to be heard.

"The problem is," he said more firmly, "You're so caught up in trying not to do something wrong, you don't realize that you never did anything wrong, to begin with. Your excitement and passion for the people you love is admirable and rare. It's wonderful, and if someone doesn't like it, then they're crazy."

"What are you trying to say, Daniel?"

He brushed my crazy hair from my face and grazed his thumbs over my cheeks, rendering me immobile. "I'm saying you don't have to be so defensive. I love your personality. I just don't like being woken up at two in the morning. Next time, write down what you need to tell me, and call me or come by at a normal hour. You can go bananas overboard, and I'd love it... just... you know, not when I'm asleep."

I sighed and rubbed my temples. "I'm sorry. I'm so messed up. Ronin was right, I'm just too much to handle sometimes. I don't think about what I'm doing most of the time. I'm exhausting and overbearing and clingy and—"

"Perfect. You're perfect exactly how you are, Peaches, and I really want to kiss you right now." He interrupted my sentence, then leaned in and hovered over my lips. "Would that be okay with you?"

I lost my breath, but I needed to know one crucial bit of information before I nodded frantically. "We've kissed before. Why ask now?"

"Because those kisses were to make Ronin jealous. This one, it's only for me."

I nodded, and he pressed his lips to mine. It was calm and gentle, slow, and filled with more emotion than any kiss I'd ever shared with anyone. It wasn't just a kiss, not simple physical affection—it was a connection with him that I had never had with anyone else, a place I felt safe and... *loved.* And it scared me.

I pulled away gently. "Daniel, I'm... this is..."

"It's okay. I know. Me too," he whispered, gently peppering my face with little kisses. "For the record, I didn't plan this part."

"Plan what part?" I whispered in kind, still rattled from what had just happened.

His eyes made direct contact with mine, darted around my face looking for something, then settled back on my eyes. "You don't know? After everything, after that kiss you still don't know?"

I shook my head, then remembered our deal. His kiss had all but made me forget about our deal and Ronin, the reason we became friends to begin with. "Oh, the Ronin deal. Um... yeah."

He chuckled. "No, not the Ronin and Sara plan, Hazel. My plan with you."

"Me?" I asked, still confused and in a daze. "What plan, Daniel? What are you talking about?"

He dropped his arms to his sides. "For crying out loud, Hazel, I love you."

Fifteen

I gazed into his eyes and noticed just how much could be read in the tones of green and gold—appreciation, trust, hope, amazement, joy, fear, and hiding just behind the beautiful golden tones that faded into the green—love. It was more than I'd ever read in Ronin's eyes, more than I'd read in anyone's for that matter, and it scared the snot out of me. He didn't give me much time to contemplate his confession before going on.

"Screw Ronin. He messed up, screw him. He let you go, but I would never do that, Hazel. I would never, ever let you go," he said. Those eyes. They showed so much emotion, now practically begging me to choose him over anyone else.

"Daniel, I—"

"Hazel, just give me a chance. That's all I'm asking for. This whole get back at Ronin plan was the only way I could get you to see me. Really see me, and not just as some random guy you—"

"Wait, are you saying this whole thing was a set-up to get closer to me?" I asked, my heart dropping as I waited for him to confirm what I already knew. He lied to me. I always thought, of everyone I knew, that Daniel would never lie to me.

"I..." He dropped his hands to his sides in defeat. "Yes. I've liked you for a long time, but—"

"How could he have liked me for a long time when you didn't even know me? When we kissed after the fire alarm, you said I was a random stranger. That was the first lie, wasn't it? And then the plan. You lied when you said you wanted to help me get Ronin back."

"Not entirely. It's what you wanted, and I wanted you to be happy. If the plan had worked, I would have walked away," he said. "That's the truth. With Ronin or with me, all I wanted was for you to be happy."

"Why? Why didn't you just tell me the truth?"

"I was scared! There you were, this girl I'd liked for over a year, asking me to kiss her. I freaked out, said stupid crap, then went and made a fool of myself with this stupid plan. But I swear, Peaches, if things had worked out with Ronin, I would have walked away again."

"Again? Daniel, you're not making any sense." I said. "How can you like someone for over a year that you don't know a thing about?" My heart screamed *why does it matter? You love him, too!* But my mind fought against my heart in a tug of war. *He lied and tricked you.*

"I had to get to know you, so I wouldn't get you a bad gift for Secret Valentine. I had no idea who you were until I drew your name, but after, when I took the time to figure you out..." He hesitated, then hit it home. "I saw you, Peaches, who you really are, and I wanted to keep getting to know you. I wanted to be with you. I still do, and unless I'm stupid, I think you want to be with me, too."

"I don't understand why you didn't just tell me all this, Daniel. You had to trick me into getting close to you. Do you know how that makes me feel? Like an idiot, that's how," I argued.

"Peaches, I'm sorry. That wasn't my intention at all, I just..."
He threw his hands in the air. "Look at me! In what world does
a person like you fall for a guy like me? In case you haven't
noticed, I'm a little weird."

He reached for me, but I wasn't quite there yet. I felt stupid,
like the little child he played games with. Like the little dog, he
baited with a trail of treats just to see if he could catch me.

"Peaches, can't we please forget this stupid plan ever existed?
I just want a chance to show you how much I care about you.
Give me a chance, Peaches. I'm not like him, I swear I would
never hurt you that way."

I inched away from him, needing space to clear my mind. I
left my car behind where Daniel stood. I don't know why, but
I felt I would hyperventilate if I didn't take a walk and breathe.
Deep down, I knew Daniel didn't mean to hurt me, but what he
didn't understand, what he would probably *never* understand,
was that he'd already hurt me. I trusted him implicitly. I'd never
trusted someone so much in my life, not someone I didn't share
DNA with. But our relationship, our friendship, it was all built
on a lie, a trick.

The more I inched away, the more he tried to reach me, so
I did the only thing I knew to do to get a little room to think. I
ran.

"Hazel, wait!" I heard him call after me, but I was too
distracted to listen. I continued across the street without
bothering to check both ways. No one ever drove down those
back neighborhood streets, and certainly not in the middle of
the night.

He called out again, and just as I turned to tell him to shut up
before he woke the entire neighborhood, I saw it. Two lights
growing larger by the second. I wanted to move, but my feet
were frozen in place, seemingly insistent on getting me killed. A

horn blared, and tires screeched, and still, my feet didn't move. Everything happened in slow motion, a blur in time that my brain could not comprehend.

Something shoved me hard, and I fell into the shrubs on the opposite side of the road. Whoever's roses I destroyed would be plenty angry in the morning, but I paid for it with every tear in my skin. A car door slammed, and someone yelled, "Somebody call 911!" as they hunched over a body in the middle of the road.

I scanned the area for Daniel, but I didn't see him. It's funny, all the ways your brain will try to tell you everything is just fine when it knows it's not. I looked for him everywhere, never once considering that *he* was the body in the middle of the road until the driver of the car turned him to his back.

He lay in a lump on the ground, his face bloody, and his eyes closed. I heard sirens in the distance, but my brain shut them out. I saw the lights flashing and people running around, but my mind blocked them as well. A paramedic spoke to me, but I didn't hear the words she said. All I saw was Daniel's limp body placed on a stretcher, then hoisted into the back of an ambulance.

The doors slammed, and the ambulance took off, then it all came to me in a rush. The sirens, the flashing lights, the sounds of the driver crying, the paramedic trying to gain my attention—everything came rushing into my brain and crashed into an explosion of noise that was nearly deafening.

"Daniel!" I screamed and ran after the ambulance.

I was stopped by a hand on my shoulder. I whirled around to find a police officer doing his best to keep me from running down the street like a mad woman. "Miss, I'm sorry. I need your help. I need to call his parents. We need a number if you have one."

"Uh... um... S-sure..." I gave them the number to his mother's cell phone, the one she insisted I use if I ever needed anything. "I... Can I go now?" I was dazed and confused, but I needed to get to the hospital as soon as possible.

"Is there someone you can call to take you? I won't let you drive in this state," the officer insisted. I wondered why he was so mean, but I accepted he wouldn't let me leave alone. I decided to call my mother, which meant I was in for the punishment of a lifetime—as if Daniel getting hit by a car wasn't the worst punishment in the world. Dad was at work, and it gave me a slight peace of mind to know my father would take care of Daniel—but not much.

My mother answered after three rings, her voice groggy. "Hazel? Where are you?"

"Mom, I need your help," I sobbed into the phone. "It's Daniel, he's in the hospital, and—"

"I'm on my way. Where are you?" She was wide awake now, and I heard shuffling in the background.

"His house. Hurry, mom," I continued to cry, praying he wasn't dead. It was all my fault. If I'd just listened to him, he'd be okay. If I had only talked things out with him, then he wouldn't be on his way to the hospital.

When she arrived, she didn't lecture or yell at me, she only drove as quickly as she could to the hospital without breaking any laws. There would be time for grounding and yelling later; for now, she was just as concerned as I was.

Dad met us at the door, stopping me before I went nuts, searching every room for him. "Honey, he's going to be fine. Calm down."

"I want to see him!" I yelled. "Daniel!"

My father gripped my arms tightly and held me still. "Young lady, you're in enough trouble as it is. Do not make it worse by disobeying hospital rules," he said firmly. "Calm yourself, and I'll take you to see him. After that... I don't even know how much trouble you'll be in, but I promise you, it'll be college before you see another face besides your mother's and mine."

"Did you get his mother, dear?" my mother asked, easing the edge on my father's anger.

"I did. She's on her way back, but it's going to be at least six hours," Dad replied. "I'm not concerned, though. I'm not allowed to divulge his injuries, I can say, it could have been much worse," he said, giving me a disapproving glare.

"Can I go in now, please?" I asked in a much more controlled manner. I didn't care if I was grounded until I was forty; I just needed to know Daniel was okay.

"Yes, room four, but only a few minutes," Dad said, pointing down the hall.

I knocked on the glass door, gaining Daniel's attention. He turned his head to face me, but when he saw it was me, he turned back the other way. No smile, no smart remark... nothing. I couldn't shake the feeling that even though he was sitting right there, I'd killed my best friend—on the inside, at least.

"Daniel?" I entered the room and closed the door behind me. "How are you feeling?"

"Like I got hit by a car, Hazel. How do you think?" he snapped.

"I'm sorry, Daniel, I didn't mean for—"

"You never do, do you? You never mean for things to go wrong, but they do, and now I'm stuck in a hospital bed after getting hit by a freaking car, Hazel!" he shouted.

"It was an accident. How was I supposed to know this was going to happen?" I asked, wringing my hands.

"It was a street! How do you not know cars drive in the street?" he asked, his good arm flailing. The other was wrapped in a soft cast.

"That's not fair. You know what I meant, Daniel. I'm not stupid," I defended.

"I know you're not stupid, Hazel. I'm sorry, but I can't talk to you right now. Please leave," he snapped. *Hazel.* No Peaches. Of all the things I did to Ronin, at least I never got him hit by a car. Why didn't I just let it go? Why did I have to make a big deal out of his confession? It's not like he intentionally hurt me for fun. The point was that he loved me. Maybe he did some idiotic things to get my attention, but in the end, it was obvious Daniel was a good person who made a mistake—something I had done a thousand times.

"Why?" I asked, more to myself than him, but he responded anyway.

"I need some space, please. I need space because I told you I loved you, and all you could see was the mistake I made. You ran away instead of talking to me, and I swear, Hazel, I've never felt more rejected in my life, so please just go."

"But Daniel, I—"

"Hazel, please leave," he said, exhausted.

I backed up right into the door, forgetting I'd closed it. My back ached from the fall, but I couldn't stop staring at the boy in the bed—the one who refused to look at me. I saw my reflection in the mirror over the sink. My face was scratched and bloody from the thorns on the rose bushes, and I'd forgotten my hair was shorter. It all came crashing down, everything that had gone wrong from the very beginning with the balloons, and I ran from the room crying.

Days passed with no word from Daniel. He was recovering at home, but that was all my father would tell me. It was all he could legally tell me, but it wasn't enough. The days without him were bleak, and though everyone tried, no one could get through my hardened exterior. I missed three cheer practices, failed my calculus test, and avoided my sister and friends like the plague.

Rose tried to get me to talk, but I locked her out of my room every day after school, and I didn't come out until morning. I fought the urge to text Daniel a million times. He wanted space, and I knew suffocating him with messages was not the answer. Dizzy cracked jokes on the way to school, all for my benefit, but nothing got through. I was a zombie, going through the motions until Tee took matters into his own hands. What he did probably wouldn't make a lot of sense to most people, but it turned out to be the best way to deal with my retreat into misery. Tee chose the nuclear option. He sent Ronin.

"I figured I'd find you here," Ronin's deep voice cut through my self-induced catatonic state, slumped over a book, hiding under the bleachers on the soccer field.

"What do you want?" I spat, not quite in the mood to deal with him.

"Just to talk, that's all," he said, sitting on the ground beside me.

"Well, this isn't awkward at all." I sighed.

"It doesn't have to be, Hazel. It's just two people who have known each other for a long time, having a conversation."

"You ruined my self-esteem and humiliated me in front of the entire school. Why would I want to talk to you?" I spat again, not even recognizing the person I'd become in only a few days without Daniel in my life.

"I'm sorry about how that all happened, Hazel. I really am. I love how supportive and caring you are and how you always cheered the loudest when I was on the field. I love how you helped me with schoolwork and anything else I needed. You were great as a girlfriend, but..." he hesitated, taking in the evil glare focused on him. Even so, he chose to continue.

"But... sometimes you'd go overboard, at least in my opinion, and those were the things I couldn't handle. I'm a private person, and you, well, you're a thundering herd of horses in a china shop—beautiful and awe-inspiring, but not exactly quiet. I was wrong to hurt you the way I did. I should have broken up with you in private and explained things better. I hope you believe me when I say I really regret the way everything happened."

I sighed, admitting that he wasn't all wrong, at least not from his own perspective. "It's not like you're the first person to tell me that. I messed up, too. I know that, but I don't know how to be any other way."

"You shouldn't have to change for anyone, Hazel. I'm sorry I made you feel like it was all you. It wasn't. It was mostly me because I should have known when we got together it might end this way. You were just... impossible to ignore. You're something else, and I thought I would be okay with that, that I could handle the things you do, but I'm not that guy. None of that matters though because Daniel loves you just how you are," he said.

"How do you know he loves me?" I asked.

"I'm pretty sure him threatening to smash my face in if I hurt you again would be a good clue for anyone," he said, chuckling.

"He did that?"

"Yeah, for you. You are the best, Hazel. I miss you like crazy, but I know I'm not right for you. And if you smack me with one of those Sara comments right now, I'll scream. Honestly, I never liked her when we were dating either. It's like she got some sick enjoyment out of seeing you fail."

"She is a horrible person. She's the reason I have this fabulous new haircut." I said.

"Well, you still look gorgeous with short hair, so it's not a big deal." He laughed and said, "In all seriousness, Hazel, I know you were trying to make me jealous, and it worked. Just because

I don't want to date you anymore doesn't mean all the good memories just go away. It doesn't mean I don't hate seeing you with someone else, but in the long run, it's the right thing. He loves you just the way you are. That's something I can't do, Hazel. I want to, but we aren't compatible, and I'll always want you to change things about yourself that are core to who you are. That's not fair to you, and that's why I really broke up with you. I'd really like to be your friend because you're perfect for me in that way, but Daniel—he's the one who deserves your love. I never did."

"I do love him," I admitted. "I love him so much, but I screwed it up."

"I doubt you screwed it up beyond repair, Hazel. Those feelings don't just disappear overnight, so tell him."

"I don't know how to fix it, Ronin. I got him hit by a car, you realize that, right?"

"I'm suddenly grateful I only fell in ice cream cake," he joked.

"I'm serious, Ronin. I can't fix this," I said.

"Sure you can, Hazel." He stood and took my hand, pulling me to my feet. "You go do what you do best. Go big or go home."

Sixteen

"Of all people, you're the last one I'd expect to help me with this," I said, scrolling through the options on the website.

"I still care about you, and I want you to be happy, Hazel. You know, there were about a dozen times I almost broke down and begged you to take me back," Ronin said, looking over my shoulder. "Here, that's it. That's the one I was telling you about."

I clicked on the link, and the page loaded. "Why didn't you? Out of curiosity, I mean."

"What? And try to compete with Casanova himself?" Ronin teased.

"I wouldn't call Daniel Casanova," I chuckled and looked over the choices. "This package looks good. I can print the map now and just give him the official one when it comes in."

"Yeah, I think that will work. He'll get the point," Ronin said, checking the printer for paper. "As far as calling him Casanova, all I'll say is from the outside looking at the two of you, it was pretty obvious there's crazy chemistry there. You never looked like that after I kissed you."

His tone was a little saddened. "I'm sorry, Ronin. It's not like—"

"No, no, no, Hazel. I don't want you to be sorry. I meant what I said; I don't think we're a good match as more than friends. It's just an adjustment, you know?"

I nodded. "Yeah, I do, and I'm glad we can talk now. I'd miss you a lot if we couldn't at least be friends."

I glanced around Ronin's bedroom, a place I used to spend a lot of time. It didn't feel quite as comfortable any longer, and my interaction with Ronin didn't give me the flutters it once did. It felt like we were just friends like it did way back at the beginning. He pulled the sheet from the printer and handed it to me. I rolled it up and tucked it into my purse, ready for phase two.

"Are you sure you're up for helping with this part?" I asked, not wanting to rub salt in the wound.

"Absolutely. The others will meet us there," Ronin said. "Come on, let's go fix this mess." He wrapped his arm over my shoulders and squeezed, his bright blue eyes happy again. I hadn't seen them that way since before the balloon fiasco.

He drove us to the beach, where my sister, Tee, and Dizzy waited. Tee agreed to let me borrow his telescope, and since I had no idea how to work it, he also decided to find the particular star I wanted. The telescope was much larger than I'd anticipated. I sure hoped Daniel would forgive me because lugging that thing back to my car by myself would be misery.

Rose brought the food and picnic supplies I'd requested. Somehow, Dizzy managed to find an exact replica of the old man bear from the bookstore—that, or she swiped him from his chair at the store, thereby freeing him from the monotony of Curious George.

Rose handed me a giant stick. "Here, I think you should do the honors yourself."

I took the stick and searched the shoreline for the best place—somewhere the wind wouldn't destroy my work, and the water wouldn't erase it. I found a small alcove, a secluded little spot behind a small outcropping of rocks.

"That's a perfect spot," Rose said, then she and Dizzy set up the supplies. The sun was setting, so we had to work fast. Tee finished setting up the telescope while I wrote the last bit of my message in the sand. Ironically, neither Rose nor Dizzy questioned Ronin's presence, both accepting that we had managed to settle our issues once and for all. Ronin was a big help, and his admission that we simply weren't right for each other was spot-on even if it did hurt a little. He'd given me something—closure. Little did Ronin know I had a surprise in store for him, too.

"When does it start?" Tee asked.

I checked my phone. "About an hour until the eclipse begins, so we've got a little time left," I said.

"I don't think so." Tee pointed up the shore toward a towering boy wandering alone on the beach.

"Poo," Dizzy said. "You go talk to him, and we'll finish here."

"Are you sure?" I asked.

"Go!" they all shouted at once as they scrambled to set up the candles and arrange blankets and pillows.

I did as told and climbed over the rocks that blocked my surprise from view. It was dark now, but the eclipse hadn't started, so the moon was bright enough to illuminate the shore. I knew it was Daniel without even seeing his face. I knew it from the way he stood, the way he walked, the way he brushed his fingers through his hair.

"Fancy meeting you here," I said as I walked up to him. My heart thudded so hard I thought it might explode out of my chest like one of those cartoon characters in love.

"Hazel, what are you doing here?" Daniel asked. I flinched when I saw his arm. The cast was a sad reminder of what tore us apart before we even got started.

"Please don't call me that," I begged, choking back tears that would ruin what I had planned.

"It is your name. You said so yourself," he said. He wasn't the snappy Daniel from the hospital, not cold or aloof, but distant enough that it broke my heart. Debating my name was not worth the time, not when I had so many other things that needed to be said.

"Can we talk? We have time, like forty-five minutes before the penumbral starts," I asked.

"The penumbral? Someone's been studying her astronomy. I mean, it's not exactly right, but... it's a nice effort," he said, a lighter tone that gave me hope.

"Oh, I thought... I looked it all up after you asked me to watch it with you, but I won't lie. I didn't understand half of it. I guess I didn't want to look stupid in front of you, which is basically impossible since, you know..." I waved my hand, indicating I knew I'd never reach his level of intelligence, not by a long shot.

"Please don't do that. You're so smart, Hazel, and if I only hung out with people as smart as me, I'd be bored to tears. Besides, I wasn't too smart when it came to you, was I?" He sat down, patting the sand beside him. I sat cautiously, too afraid to hope it could be this easy.

"I'm sorry I got so upset. I was shocked and hurt that you lied to me, but I should have given you a chance to argue your side," I admitted. "I should have just heard you out."

"I should have told you the truth from the beginning, the real beginning, and maybe things would be different now. Maybe we'd be together, but now..." he trailed, staring out over the crashing waves. "I'm not mad anymore, so maybe we can fix our friendship somehow? I mean, if that's why you're here. I'd like that. I miss bantering with you."

"I'm not here to fix our friendship, Daniel," I started.

"Oh, I just assumed that's why you came. I guess it would be a little weird for us to hang out after I confessed that I love you," he said, still refusing to look at me. If he did, maybe he'd see the answer to his question instead of doubting my feelings.

"Will you walk with me for a minute? I just want to show you something real quick. Only take a minute," I said. He glanced at me, but it was too dark to see his eyes, leaving me with very little to gauge his emotions.

"Sure, where to my lady?" Old Daniel was in there somewhere, and I wanted him back more than I could ever explain. I'd have to do what I did best, just as Ronin said. *Go big, or go home, Hazel.* He followed me down the beach to the rocks. I slipped my shoes off so I could climb the rocks better, all the while Daniel watched.

"Is that a good idea? You're fairly uncoordinated for a cheer captain," he teased.

"I've got it. I'm all good. Let's go, Daniel, before... Oh, wow." Even I hadn't seen the finished product. I had some incredible friends, and I'd have to work hard to show them how much I appreciated them, but at that moment, all I could do was take in the scene.

"What the..." Daniel stood beside me on the rocks, gazing out over the private area my friends had made for us. The girls went overboard with the candles, but it was beautiful. Easily a hundred flickered in the darkness, illuminating a pathway to the picnic. There were cushions and pillows, a comfortable little space for eating, and watching an eclipse for hours.

I hopped down to the sand, turning to see if he would follow. Daniel's eyes were locked on something, so he barely paid any attention to me. I followed his gaze, settling on the words I'd written in the sand.

"Is this for me? Did you do all this for me?" he asked.

I nodded, then remembered he wasn't paying any attention to me. "Yes," I whispered, unable to vocalize anything louder. I was terrified, shaking in the sand, waiting for his response.

He hopped down and walked over to the message, the giant letters carved out in the sand that said *I love you* yet didn't feel like enough to relay the way I felt about him.

"You love me?" he asked, skeptical at best, as he pointed to the message.

"I do," I said.

"Oh."

I waited for more, but all he did was walk closer to my declaration written in the sand where anyone could see. He walked around it, staring at the words as if he'd never seen them written before.

"So... What does this mean? Are you... are *we* on the same page?" he asked, looking back up at me. I could see the worry on his face, illuminated by the flickering candles. I walked over to him and took his hand.

I slid mine comfortably into his. "If that's what you want, yes. I meant what I wrote here, Daniel. I love you, and I hope you can forgive me because I want very much to be your girlfriend."

"I love you, too," he said, allowing me to relax a little. "I love you, and I want that more than anything."

"I'm a lot of work, Daniel. I do a lot of crazy things, and you say it's fine, but I can promise I will embarrass you one day," I reminded him.

"You're worth it, and you're crazy if you don't know that by now." He pulled me closer, wrapped his arms around my shoulders, and tucked me against his chest.

"I love you, Daniel."

"I love you, too, Peaches." I sighed, finally feeling whole again.

"So, is this it? Are we really doing this? Is this day one of Hazel and Daniel taking over the world?" I asked, just to be sure before I did my happy dance.

"Yeah, I think it is," he smiled. "But... That whole balloon thing you did for Ronin on your first anniversary, can we not do that?"

"You mean recreating how we got together? You said it wasn't a big deal, and he was an idiot for getting mad about it," I said.

"Don't get me wrong, I think it was a sweet thing you did, but I don't want to get hit by a car every year."

I laughed so hard I shook, then laughed more when he tried to laugh through busted ribs and snorted. "How about this, why don't we skip the whole getting hit by the car part, and just call this moment right now our moment?" I asked.

"I don't know, Peaches. It doesn't feel all that epic."

"Are you kidding me? It took forever to plan this and—"

"I'm just trying to get you to kiss me, Peaches," he said. He leaned down and did just that, creating a puddle of Hazel again. I knew, at that moment, that I would be mopping myself up for the rest of my life. I couldn't imagine being any happier with anyone else. He broke the kiss, a little short for my taste, but he had something to say.

"I need to tell you something, then I'm going to ask you a really, really selfish question, Peaches. Is that okay?" he asked.

"You don't have a selfish bone in your body, Daniel, but go ahead," I said, pulling him over to the picnic area so I could give him his other surprise once he was finished.

He licked his lips and took a breath. He was nervous, and it was adorable. "I love you, Hazel Simmons. I love you so much, I can't breathe when I think about leaving you behind after summer. I want you to come with me if you can. Please come with me, Peaches."

My eyeballs nearly bugged out of my head, but I found my heart screaming at me to *just say yes!* However, my parents had grounded me for all eternity, so I decided to be somewhat reasonable and get the details first. "You want me to go with you to... Wait, where are you going?"

"The program is in D.C., but after that, I'm not sure. It all depends on how that goes, but maybe anywhere, depending on college. So, you see, it really is a selfish request, but—"

"Okay." I was sure of it. It was what I wanted, and there were plenty of colleges in the D.C. area I could apply to.

"Okay, you understand the question, and you'll think about it, or okay, you'll go?" he asked, giving me a skeptical look again.

"Okay, I'll go with you. I have a good idea of what I want to do with my life now, and I feel certain I can find a school that will fit my needs. Yeah... Yes, Daniel. I want to go to D.C. with you."

"I can't believe you said yes." He sighed and fell back onto the pillows. "I thought for sure... I'm so happy right now."

"Look, Daniel," I said, pointing up at the moon. "It's starting."

He sat up and looked at the moon. "I love watching a lunar eclipse, especially with you here, but I have a question."

"What's that?" I asked, watching as the first bit of shadow cast over the moon.

"Why is there a telescope? We don't need it for the eclipse, Peaches."

"Oh!" I said. "I almost forgot." I pulled the rolled-up sheet of paper from my purse and handed it to him. "We don't need it for the eclipse, but we do need it for this."

He unrolled the paper and read it. "You named a star for me, Peaches? You literally named it Daniel's Peach. I love it, really.

It's the best gift I've ever gotten," he said, leaning in to kiss me again.

It was the best moment of my life—and cue the fireworks. Literal, real fireworks. It turned out I'd taught my friends a thing or two about over the top gestures, and they gave me a magical evening in return. Gorgeous colors exploded in the air as the shadow continued its passing over the moon.

I snuggled in next to Daniel to watch the show. I chuckled a little, thinking of our situation.

"What's so funny, Peaches?"

"I can't believe my best friend is my boyfriend," I said.

"Aw, see baby, we're a walking cliché category after all," he teased, hugging me tightly as we shut out the rest of the world.

Seventeen

"So, this isn't strange at all," Daniel said, looking between Ronin and me.

"You have nothing to worry about, Daniel. I love you, remember?" I told him. I hadn't put much thought into how prom would go, but I believed Daniel was adult enough to put aside his differences with Ronin just as I was.

"Still super weird," Daniel said, giving Ronin one last once over.

"It's like I told Hazel, it doesn't have to be weird. We've all moved on, and she's happy with you," Ronin said.

"What are you talking about?" Daniel asked.

Ronin tilted his head to the side, the thing he always did when he was thoroughly confused. "All of us sharing a limo to prom? You're feeling awkward about it, right?"

"No, I was talking about the tux. It's super weird, like, how the heck does it go on? There are so many pieces!" Daniel said, holding up the jacket to inspect the pockets.

I breathed a sigh of relief. When Rose first broached the subject of sharing a limo to prom, I was hesitant to agree because

M. J. PADGETT

I didn't want Daniel to feel, well, weird. With Tee taking Rose and him being Ronin's best friend, I didn't want our history to determine how much fun we could have at prom. Ronin and I were still connected in so many ways, and it didn't seem fair to make anyone choose who they wanted to spend time with.

"I told you both, I don't care if you're friends. I trust my Peaches, and I'll still kill you if you hurt her. As long as you know those two things, we're good. Now, someone tell me how to tie this thing," Daniel groaned, tossing the tie at me.

"I don't know how to do it. Don't look at me!" I said, earning a groan from my mother.

"Honestly, you children know nothing. Give it to me." She took the tie and quickly tied it into a neat bow with deft fingers. Daniel's eyes grew large and shocked.

"Honey, you're killing the boy. Let me do it," my father said, taking over where my mother left off. "She used to tie mine so tight I couldn't breathe, and I'd have to sneak away to loosen it."

"You never told me that!" Mom fussed.

"Didn't want to hurt your feelings or get myself killed. There we go, all set." Dad patted Daniel's shoulder, then my mother corralled us all in for pictures.

Daniel draped his arm over me and pulled me close to whisper in my ear, "You have to tell them soon, Peaches."

I nodded, but I wasn't about to tell my parents I was moving to D.C. an hour before my senior prom, especially when it would take that long to explain how I came to that decision in the first place. "Tomorrow, I promise."

Tee wrapped his arm around Rose as my mother snapped photo after photo. Ronin stood off to the side, a little lonely and sad without a date—that he knew of, anyway. Daniel noticed the same time I did and said, "Hey, let's get a group photo."

Ronin seemed pleased to be a part of the group, but I hoped he liked the girl I talked into going to prom with a boy she didn't know, as a favor to me, another person she hardly knew. Dizzy, who decided prom wasn't all that bad of an idea when the right person asked her to go, wandered into the room, finally finished with her make-up.

It so happened, pink stripe girl who rescued me from Sara, sat behind Dizzy and Rose in one of their classes. She—Amelia—overheard quite a bit of juicy gossip. When Sara attacked me in the hall, Amelia felt compelled to stick up for me—that, and her brother was crazy head over heels for Dizzy. Through a series of complicated and comedic notes passed through Amelia, her brother—Aiden—convinced Dizzy to go to prom with him. A lot happened behind the scenes while I was spiraling, but it turned out spectacularly in the end.

"This is so fun. Your parents are so funny," Aiden said, glancing at Dizzy, who blushed—blushed!

"Don't tell them that, or Dad will start telling you terrible doctor jokes," I said, jumping when the doorbell rang.

"Who could that be?" Mom asked.

Daniel was the only other person who knew what I'd done since he'd been present through the entire ten minutes of begging I had to do to convince Natalie to go to prom—again. Been there, done that was her excuse. To Natalie, it was as good an excuse as any, but I wouldn't have it. I convinced her that a nineteen-year-old most certainly could go to prom again, and no one would know her anyway. For some reason, the girl took pity on me and agreed—which meant I owed her for the slushy on Sara's head *and* suffering through a prom she wasn't keen on attending.

"I got it!" I said, rushing to the door. Natalie looked beautiful, and I knew Ronin would like her. I already thought she was great, and she was the kind of girl I imagined Ronin would like in the long run. She spoke her mind, but she was subtle and understated. Fun and smart, and an avid soccer player—all of which I learned after she finally agreed to go.

"You made it! I'm so glad you didn't change your mind!" I said, ushering her in.

"I made a promise, Hazel. I don't go back on my word," she said with a smile. "Besides, I guess it could be fun."

I escorted her into the living room, where everyone else was patiently waiting, including her date for the night. Ronin's eyes met hers, and his jaw dropped a little. "Hey, you're slushy girl!"

"And you're the jerky ex-boyfriend with bad taste in rebounds!" she said, pointing at him.

"And you're each other's date for prom! Yay!" I said. I clapped my hands and pretended the tension didn't exist. "Ronin, this is Natalie. Natalie, Ronin, and just to clarify, we're friends. Long story, but oh, look at the time! We need to go!"

I grabbed Daniel's arm and dragged him out the door where the limo was just pulling up. "Your girlfriend is insane, you know that, right?" Ronin said to Daniel.

"Yep. And she's all mine, no takesies backsies, sorry." Daniel shrugged and opened the door for me.

The ride to prom was very civil, and Natalie and Ronin got to know each other a little better on the way. I would never have expected my senior year to end the way it did, with a brand new boyfriend, plans to move to D.C., new friends, and back to being friends with Ronin, but it was a pretty cool way to end the year. And if we won regionals, it would only be icing on the cake—the non-ice cream kind.

"You look really beautiful," Daniel said for the tenth time.

"Thank you. You clean up pretty nice yourself."

"I hate this tux," he admitted like it was surprising news. "I feel like old man bear, stuck inside, screaming to get out."

"Well, you've got a few hours of torture ahead of you, sorry," I said, sliding out of the seat once the driver had parked. Daniel wasted no time removing me from the company of our friends and pulled me along the walkway to the pond behind the event center.

"What are you doing?" I asked. "We have to check in at the front desk."

"I know. I just wanted to give you something." He pulled a box from his pocket and handed it to me. "I wrapped it myself."

"I can tell," I said, trying to find a place that didn't have tape on it. I finally spied a tiny corner that was peelable and ripped it open. Inside was a pendant with an unusual-looking stone.

"It's beautiful, Daniel. What is it?" I asked.

"It's a moonstone, so whenever you look at it, you'll be reminded of our first official date," he said, clasping the pendant around my neck.

"You know, you're kind of an amazing boyfriend, Daniel."

"Amazing enough that we can skip prom and hang at the bookstore?" he asked with a joking tone. I looked down at my dress, then back to him. I felt fine, but he was horribly uncomfortable. I knew he would suffer through it for me, but I was starting to feel like doing something else, something with fewer people and more Daniel.

"I think so, come on!" I grabbed his hand and dragged him back toward the limo.

"Hazel, we can't skip prom. You've been looking forward to it for... I don't know, forever," he shouted but didn't fight me all that much.

"Hey, where are you guys going?" Rose shouted when I jerked open the limo door.

"Cake, ice cream, and dusty old books!" I yelled. Daniel slid in beside me and told the driver where to take us. He drove away, leaving six confused people behind, but they would be just fine without us. The driver passed our place, and I started to speak up, but Daniel shushed me.

"Patience grasshopper, for I have a surprise for thee," he said.

"You're so weird," I said, settling back in. The driver pulled into the school parking lot and parked beside the practice field.

"Thank you. We won't be long," Daniel said, handing the driver extra cash for his trouble.

"What are we doing here?" I asked.

"I said I have a surprise, Peaches. Just wait for it." He led me down the walkway to the field, just off the sideline in the middle. It was the place where I'd grabbed him and asked him to kiss me.

He turned around and said, "Right here."

"Right here what?"

"Right here is where you made me question everything I wanted for my future, Peaches. My plan was to finish high school and get out of here, on to bigger and better things. But you went and pulled that crazy stunt with the fire alarm—"

"You saw that?"

"I did. You're not as sneaky as you think you are. Be glad Mr. Overton likes me, or you'd have been suspended."

"He saw too?"

"Not the point here, Peaches. The point is, you did what you did, and I suddenly saw this second chance to get your attention. See, I had accepted that you were with someone better than me, and I moved on, so to speak. Then, of all the people you could have snatched up in that field, you chose me."

"I'm glad I chose you. Turned out to be the best accidental choice of my life," I said.

"Well, I wanted you to know it was this spot, this very spot, that I realized I wanted more from life than just an awesome job. I want a wife and kids, a stupid minivan and a mortgage, and all the other things you get when you love someone. I mean, not right now, but in the future and all with you."

"Do we have to get a minivan? Maybe an SUV instead?" I teased.

"Whatever you want, Peaches, as long as it's parked in a garage next to mine," he said.

"Throw in a couple of dogs, and you've got yourself a deal, Daniel," I said.

"Promise?" he asked with a tone of longing.

"I promise. Why so sad?"

"Because I've been thinking, and it was really unfair of me to ask you to walk away from everything and everyone you love to follow me to D.C. I think you should do what you want for school first. We can survive a long-distance relationship, I'm sure of it."

"Daniel—"

"Let me finish, or I'll back out. I don't want you to look back and have doubts or wonder if you should have—"

"Daniel, shh. For once, just close your yapper and listen to me. I'm going with you to D.C., and I've already enrolled in a school there. It was supposed to be a surprise for later, but I've decided what I want to do with my life."

"Really? Care to share that with me, Peaches?" he asked with a ridiculously adorable grin.

"Event planning, large scale, big time. Celebrities will beg me to plan their events, Daniel," I said, imagining it as I said it.

"Perfect. I think that's perfect, Peaches. I love you, and I can't wait," he said. "Ready for our place now?"

"Yeah, let's go. We won't have much time to hang there with exams and regionals coming up. I'm gonna miss that dusty old place," I said.

We gave the limo driver a break and walked the five blocks to the bookstore without my shoes on, of course, because who could walk that far in stick-thin heels? When we stepped inside, the cranky old checkout lady smiled.

"What on earth? Did you two get lost on your way to the ball?" she asked.

"No, ma'am, we decided to skip prom and hang out here. We like it better here," Daniel said.

"You two are so adorable," she said, then disappeared into the back. Within minutes, the lights dimmed, and the music changed to something soft and slow. The children's reading area lit up with twinkle lights, and I noticed old man bear was different. I gasped when I approached and saw he was dressed in a little teddy bear tuxedo.

"You did this, too?" I asked.

"Mmmmaybe..." he said and offered his hand. "You never did give me formal dance lessons, so I'm gonna step all over your feet."

"I don't care, this is the sweetest thing anyone has ever done for me. How did you know I'd agree to leave prom?" I asked, taking his hand as I fell into his embrace.

"I wasn't sure you would, but just in case you did, I went ahead with the plan. I wanted to give you something you would never forget, not just a usual prom. And just to make this super corny and over the top, I got you this." He handed me another box. Inside was a key. I looked up at him, confused.

"For our apartment. Two bedrooms so your parents might not kill me, and right in the middle of the action. We can walk to almost anything, and if we can't walk, the train is two blocks away." My eyes bulged, and I was a little freaked out.

"How much is the rent, Daniel? I could be wrong, but I'm guessing the program doesn't pay much, and I'll be in school."

"It doesn't pay anything, but that's not a problem. Grandparents, Peaches, remember? Raised a crappy kid, ran out on us, they buy my love with crap? Well, they own the complex, so... penthouse for us."

"The... did you say penthouse?"

"Do you take issue with using an elevator daily? Because they have stairs, like a billion, but it's an option," he was mocking me, the little snot. I shoved him, but he recovered quickly. "Seriously, it has great security, and I think your parents will feel a lot better about your choice once they see where you'll be living. My grandparents live in the same building, just in another wing. What do you think?"

"Did I mention you're the best boyfriend ever?" I asked, sinking into his embrace again as he swayed to the music.

"You might have mentioned it, but it's easy for you, Peaches," he said. "Now, shall we call our friends and see if they want to join our private party?"

I looked up, gazing into his eyes. "Maybe another fifteen minutes."

He lifted me and kissed me, another of his Hazel-melting kisses, and I knew, from then on, everything would be okay. He loved me exactly how I was, over-the-top mess and all. And I loved him, the genius who cared more about helping me find my way than he did about his own happiness.

I missed being crowned prom queen, and Melanie Brockman was crowned instead. I wasn't disappointed in the least. I missed Ronin asking Natalie on another date because they had such an amazing time together. I missed my sister teaching our entire graduating class how to salsa dance. And I missed Dizzy's first kiss. I missed it all, yet I didn't miss a thing because I was exactly where I needed to be—with Daniel, the real boy I couldn't live without.

Epilogue

Seven Years Later

I tapped my fingers on the armrest, choosing to wait in the car rather than in Daniel's office. Even after seven years, I still felt like an idiot the second I passed through the door. His coworkers were friendly enough, but it was challenging to hold my own in a room filled with brilliant minds.

Staring at the door made my eyes hurt, but I couldn't look away. When Daniel emerged from the building, whatever news he had would be life-changing in one way or another. We were either staying in D.C., and Daniel would be linked to a long-term project, or we were packing and heading out on an adventure. I was nervous about both options if I'm honest, but life requires you to take the unknown and make do with what it becomes.

Rose called a dozen times, but I had no updates for her. His meeting should have ended by then, so I was far past impatient. My phone rang again, likely Rose, but I checked it anyway. I didn't recognize the number, so it was probably a potential client.

"Hello?" I asked, kicking myself for not using the professional greeting.

"Hello, is this Miss Simmons of Parties by Peaches?" a female voice asked—confident, authoritative, and hurried.

"Yes, it is. How may I help you?" I asked, crossing my fingers it was another upscale wedding or senator's birthday party.

"This is Vera McCauley. I'm calling on behalf of my client, who would like to secure your services for an upcoming event. Are you available for December 20th?" She asked.

"December 20?" I asked, glancing at my planner—two days away.

"Of next year, I should mention," she added.

"Oh, of course. I have nothing scheduled past April." I wanted to smack myself again. Way to go, Hazel, just tell everyone your schedule is wide open, and your business would probably fail before the end of the year.

"Good, don't schedule anything else. We'll need you working this event full-time," she said, but before I could tell her that wouldn't be possible—a girl can't live off the funds from one measly party—she hit me with a number that almost made me drop the phone.

"The event pays two hundred thousand, half upfront and the remainder upon delivery of service. We're prepared to give you an account with your own personal card to cover expenses and supplies; however, if you accept the job, you will be required to sign a non-disclosure agreement."

"I'm sorry, I'm confused."

"I apologize, I suppose I got a little ahead of myself didn't I?" she chuckled. "I'm just so excited you're free. I wanted to snatch you up before anyone else had the chance."

"I think you have me confused with another planner, this is Parties by Peaches, the small, one-woman operation in

Washington, D.C.," I said, fearing the worst—she'd made a huge mistake and would drop me like a bad habit when she figured it out.

"Yes, Senator Peterson recommended your services. He said his wife's fiftieth birthday party was, in his words, to die for," she said. The senator was impressed, and he promised to pass my business cards around to his friends, so perhaps this was just my lucky day.

"Oh, may I ask who is holding the event?"

"I'm sorry, that information is confidential until you sign the non-disclosure agreement, but I can assure you that you won't regret accepting the job. If the event is everything we expect it will be, you will find many more offers where this came from." Her tone was almost pleasant, far more friendly than when I first answered the phone.

"Okay, should we set an appointment to discuss the terms and details of the event?" I asked.

"Are you available in half an hour? It's short notice, but I happen to be in town for other business, and my flight leaves in three hours."

"Okay, sure. My office is on—"

"Actually, could you meet me in the lobby of the Jefferson Hotel?"

I agreed and sent Daniel a text message. His news would have to wait, but at least I had something to do to pass the time. I pulled onto the main road and headed toward the hotel, a little voice telling me this could be a prank or a crazy person, but I shook the thought from my head and drove through the traffic.

Once inside the hotel, I called Ms. McCauley. She sent me to the reception desk, where a nice young man escorted me to a conference room. Inside, Ms. McCauley hung up her cell and gave me a bright smile. She was far younger than I expected, barely older than me. She stood and rounded the table, offering me her hand.

"It's so nice to meet you, Ms. Simmons. Please, have a seat," she said, then got right down to business. "Signing the non-disclosure form does not contractually obligate you to provide your services for the event, it simply prevents you from discussing the details outside of this office, understand?" she asked, sliding the form in front of me.

I'd signed dozens of such forms before, having thrown parties for several government officials and the like. I read over the form, very standard and straightforward, then signed it. She smiled eagerly and picked up her phone.

Once someone answered the line, she said, "Come on in."

I grew nervous, but surely the hotel wouldn't send me to slaughter at the hands of a mafia man or some other crazy scary person, right? A second door in the conference room opened, and a tall, blonde-haired man entered. Once he shut the door behind him and gave me his full attention, I almost passed out.

"Hello, Ms. Simmons, my name is Justin. It's nice to meet you, and I hope I can convince you to take on my event."

"You're... you're... you're..." *Come on, Hazel, spit it out!* "You're Justin DeWalt!" I screeched.

He laughed at my reaction and said, "Indeed I am, and I'd really love to have you on board with the event. It's a celebrity auction that will benefit my farm, DeWalt Therapy Farm. Have you heard of it?"

I nodded, still unable to speak in the presence of my all-time favorite actor.

"The entire event will take place over three days, December 20 through 22, and all proceeds will go back into the farm and others like it across the country. What do you think, Ms.

Simmons, can you handle a three-day party with hundreds of celebrities?"

My jaw went slack. I was sure I hadn't blinked since Justin DeWalt entered the room. "Uh... um..."

"Don't worry, we'll help you hire an assistant or two, and you'll have your own expense account. We'll fly you in and out as necessary, but you should be able to do most of the planning from your office. Plus, as an added bonus, if you pull it off, we'll keep you on board for future events. And I'm sure I could convince my friends to hire you for their events."

"I... yes! Where do I sign?" I found my voice and screamed my answer before I lost it again.

Justin smiled happily, and his assistant shoved a contract in my face. "Look over this with your attorney, and get back to me with any questions as soon as possible. If you agree, sign it and overnight it to me. Once you do, it's all fun from here on out."

I took the stack of paperwork and slipped it into my tote, finding it difficult to tear my eyes away from the hunky actor turned advocate sitting beside me. Daniel's text message did that quite nicely, though.

"Well, we won't take any more of your time. Thank you again for coming down, Ms. Simmons." Justin offered his hand.

"Oh, please, Mr. DeWalt, call me Hazel."

"And please call me Justin. We'll be seeing a lot of each other, I hope. My wife loves your work; honestly, she threatened my life if I didn't hire you for this event," he said.

I chuckled. "Well, please give her my thanks for the endorsement."

"Will do, now if you'll excuse me, I have one last meeting before the mad dash to the airport," he said.

I barely kept it together on my way back to Danial's office, and when he met me in my car, I lost all control. "I just signed my first celebrity party," I screamed at him.

He stared blankly at me while he processed the information, then said, "Well, I hope you can work from the comfort of our new home in Hawaii."

"I'm sorry, did you say Hawaii?"

"I did, Peaches. I got the project," he added.

It was my turn to stare blankly. "I didn't know there was a project in Hawaii."

"Me either. Turns out it's a joint project with the Army, and my name was at the top of their list, so... Wanna go with me and get a nice tan?"

I jumped out of the car and met him at the back, leaping into his arms. "Yes, of course, I'm going with you! Where else would I go, doofus?"

He kissed me, and even after seven years, I was still a Hazel puddle.

"So," he finally said. "Tell me more about this event. I can't wait to hear all the details."

"If things work out, it opens doors to so much, like celebrity parties, awards shows, and, oh, I'm so excited!"

"Peaches, you're killing me! Who's it for?" he asked.

"Technically, I'm not supposed to tell you, but I might have left the contract in my tote back, just sayin'." He slid into the seat and peeked at the contract.

"Holy moly, Peaches. I'm so proud of you! I always knew you'd get this one day, and I'm so, so honored to be a part of it. You wanna go get married?"

"Huh?" I asked, shocked.

"I love you, and I promised you a lot of things seven years ago that haven't really worked out until now. It took a lot longer to get through college and secure a permanent project than I thought it would, but you followed me without hesitation, and you stayed even when it was hard. And now I'm dragging you across the country. I want to give you all the things I promised. I want to marry the most incredible person I've ever had in my life."

"I want to, Daniel, I really, really do... but... this thing will keep me so busy I'll never get a wedding planned, probably not until next year, and that's if..." I hesitated, remembering something Ronin said to me on graduation day.

You're a great person Hazel, and an even better friend. Just don't forget, sometimes it's the smaller gestures of love that mean the most.

"What's wrong, Peaches? You were doing your cute rambling thing, then you disappeared?" he asked nervously.

"Today. I can do it today. What do you think?" I asked.

"What? I can't do that to you, Peaches. You deserve a huge wedding with all your family and friends."

"It's not what I want. I've lived my life large-scale for so long, I want to let the smaller gesture prevail this time. I love you, and I want to show you how much right now." I got in the car and leaned over the console, yelling up at him. "I mean, like, right this second, Daniel. Let's go!"

He slid into the passenger seat. "Seriously? Right now?"

"Yes, but it's already four, so we have to hurry," I said, flooring the gas to get out of the crazy big parking lot.

"Wait, Peaches." I expected him to argue with me about it more, but instead, he said, "Take the next right. You'll miss the traffic from the other office and save ten minutes."

My phone rang. Rose again. "Hey, Rose, can't talk. Getting married. Gotta go, bye!" I tossed my phone into the back seat. Daniel smiled, the one I always got lost in. We made it to the courthouse just in time, got our paperwork, and hurried to fill it out, and ten minutes after we signed on the line, we were Mr. and Mrs. Starnes.

Of course, my mother made us have an official ceremony after the fact, but our elopement was symbolic in many ways. Daniel didn't care what anyone thought of him, he did his own thing and in his own time. I was a go-big or go-home kind of girl. Together, we learned what it meant to truly be loved and to love someone else—bringing all our strengths and weaknesses to the table and accepting each other for who we were. I helped Daniel connect more with the world instead of watching it from the outside, and he helped me realize the joy in the smaller things in life—both without changing a thing about each other.

Ronin McKinsey did miss me, but in the end, everything worked out the way it was supposed to. We were friends, what we should have always been. Daniel was the boy who was made for me, and when I finally realized that, everything fell into place. It wasn't always easy, but it was fun, and there was so much love. In the end, isn't that how it's supposed to be?

More In This Series

About the Author

M. J. Padgett is, first and foremost, a Christian. She is also a wife and mom. Her free-spirited daughter has quite a vivid imagination, and her antics sometimes find their way into her mommy's work. She is a lover of all things chocolate, a Grimm and Dickens addict, a self-proclaimed smarty-pants, and an introvert to the core.

Writing is her true passion (after raising her daughter, of course), and she writes as often as possible. One of her favorite things about writing is creating a world where people can escape reality for a little while, maybe even walk away feeling hopeful about the real world around them. When it comes to reading, she loves a book that can make her forget where she is, no matter the genre. If she can get lost and feel like the characters are her real friends, she's a happy reader.

Also By M. J. Padgett

MJ loves to genre hop, and you can find more to read below!

Adult & New Adult Romance and Romcoms
Life in Chatswain City Series
Home Sweet Holidays Series
The Unexpected Love Series
Merry Takes Main Street
Life with the Thomas Brothers
Dating a Denver Dragon (collaboration with Latisha Sexton and
Dulcie Dameron)

Young Adult Romance and Romcoms
The Projects of Life Trilogy
The Demolition Trilogy
I'm Pretty Sure About That Series
The Secret Author Series
100 Grand

Adult & New Adult Fantasy

Archives of the Ancient Kingdoms Series
The House of Aurum Trilogy
The McConnor & Cunningham Clock Company Series
Land of Wind and Salt

Young Adult Fantasy

Wardens of the Raven Court Series
The Immortal Grimm Brothers' Guide to Sociopathic
Princesses Series
The Wild Duology
Astryn and the Golden Goose
Love and Aliens Duology

Young Adult Sci-Fi

Journey Down Duology

Young Adult Romantic Mystery

Mattie Bender is a Cereal Killer

To find all of my books, you can search here.

Made in the USA
Monee, IL
17 November 2024

70325277R00132